Happy
Love

200 +

Newfoundland Adventures

In Air, On Land, At Sea

Other Jack Fitzgerald books

Ten Steps to the Gallows – True Stories of Newfoundland and Labrador
Treasure Island Revisited – A True Newfoundland Adventure Story
Newfoundland Disasters
Untold Stories of Newfoundland
Ghosts and Oddities
Beyond the Grave
Beyond Belief
Amazing Newfoundland Stories
Strange but True Newfoundland Stories
Newfoundland Fireside Stories
Jack Fitzgerald's Notebook
The Hangman is Never Late
Where Angels Fear to Tread
Another Time, Another Place
A Day at the Races – The Story of the St. John's Regatta
Up the Pond
Stroke of Champions
Too Many Parties, Too Many Pals
Convicted
Rogues and Branding Irons

Ask your favourite bookstore or order directly from the publisher.

Creative Book Publishing
P.O. Box 1815
367 Water Street
St. John's, NL
A1C 5P9

phone: (709) 579-1312
fax: (709) 579-6511
e-mail: nlbooks@transcontinental.ca
URL: www.creativebookpublishing.ca

Please add $5.00 Canadian for shipping and handling and taxes on single book orders and $1.00 for each additional book.

Newfoundland Adventures

In Air, On Land, At Sea

Jack Fitzgerald

CREATIVE PUBLISHERS

St. John's, Newfoundland and Labrador
2006

©2006 Jack Fitzgerald

 **Canada Council
for the Arts** **Conseil des Arts
du Canada**

 GOVERNMENT OF
NEWFOUNDLAND
AND LABRADOR

We gratefully acknowledge the financial support of The Canada Council for the Arts,
the Government of Canada through the Book Publishing Industry Development
Program (BPIDP), and the Government of Newfoundland and Labrador through the
Department of Tourism, Culture and Recreation for our publishing program.

Cover Design: Maurice Fitzgerald
Layout: Joanne Snook-Hann
Printed on acid-free paper

Published by
CREATIVE PUBLISHERS
an imprint of CREATIVE BOOK PUBLISHING
a division of Creative Printers and Publishers Limited
a Transcontinental associated company
P.O. Box 1815, Stn. C, St. John's, Newfoundland A1C 5P9

First Edition
Printed in Canada by:
TRANSCONTINENTAL PRINT

Library and Archives Canada Cataloguing in Publication
Fitzgerald, Jack, 1945-
        Newfoundland adventures / Jack Fitzgerald.

ISBN 1-897174-07-1

1. Newfoundland and Labrador--History--Anecdotes. I. Title.

FC2161.8.F555 2006   971.8   C2006-905512-2

Dedication

I dedicate this book to my second granddaughter
Eva Deirdre Fitzgerald; the latest adventure in my life.

Table of Contents

Introduction

*A*sealing vessel once competed in a cross country race against the famous 'Newfie Bullet' Train; a Newfoundland woman faces down an airline hijacker; a St. John's man, part of a commando unit, bursts into the headquarters of Hitler's top general; firefighters courageously battle a fire on a ship carrying dynamite in St. John's Harbour; a trainload of passengers becomes stranded in a terrible winter blizzard on the Gaff Topsails; and a bus driver with nerves of steel struggles to save a bus full of passengers as it speeds out of control down over Long's Hill in St. John's. These are just some of the stories the reader can look forward to reading in Jack Fitzgerald's latest book *Newfoundland Adventures: In Air, On Land At Sea.*

Chapter One is the amazing story of the Newfoundlander who was a POW in Nagasaki, Japan when the Atomic bomb was dropped.

Chapter Two tells the sad tale of the *Arctic* and the story behind why it became an embarrassment to Newfoundland. It was an event many prominent Newfoundlanders wanted forgotten. The 'Arctic Disaster' is such a compelling story that the author has chosen to delve into it much further than any other of his sea stories, and present it as a separate chapter.

Chapter Three tells the story behind how Newfoundland proved to the world the existence of the legendary 'Devil Fish' better-known today as the 'Giant Squid.' This chapter has the most extensive collection of giant squid encounter stories published to date in this province.

Chapter Four reveals some fascinating information about the old Newfoundland Railway. In addition to stories of train wrecks, trains being stranded for weeks in blizzards, and some long forgotten songs and poetry about the railway, there is the story of the cross country race between the sealing vessel *Sagona* and the 'Newfie Bullet,' and the story of how a Hollywood movie star became involved in a controversy regarding a Newfoundland Railway song. This chapter also has stories about busses out of control on St. John's hills, and the story of a terrible tragedy at a once traditional St. Paddy's Day Horse Racing event on Quidi Vidi Lake.

Chapter Five contains stories of adventure and drama in the air. These include the amazing story of the Newfoundland girl, Mary Dohey, who was instrumental in saving the lives of the passengers and crew on an Air Canada flight that had been hijacked. In another story, a plane flying over Gander faces an emergency and the courageous pilot goes through some hair-raising maneuvers to avoid disaster. A B-36 carrying an American general on a secret mission crashes near Clarenville. Stories of other airplane crashes and historic connections with Newfoundland and Labrador contribute to making this chapter fascinating reading.

Chapter Six turns to 'on land' adventures and chronicles some wonderful stories of heroism and events of worldwide interest. These include: the story of a St. John's man serving as a British commando who took part in the assault on the headquarters of General Rommel, also known as 'The Desert Fox.' Also included are the heroic stories of two Newfoundland winners of the Victoria Cross, the courageous story of Jack LeGrow of Bauline, and much more.

Chapter Seven brings together one of the most amazing collections of sea stories ever published in Newfoundland and Labrador. In addition to the story of a burning ship with a cargo of dynamite threatening St John's, and the amazing tale of Captain William Fitzgerald and the Kaiser of Germany, there is the story of a Tsunami that struck St. Shotts, on the Southern Shore of the island.

This book keeps alive so many of the wonderful stories that have contributed to Newfoundland's culture and the pride of its people. *Newfoundland Adventures* brings together an outstanding collection of stories that will inform and entertain readers for generations to come.

Chapter 1

Prisoner of War 2207

Prisoner of War 2207

*A*ugust 9, 1945, was just another routine day at Camp Fukuoka #2 in a life that had become despondent for its prisoner-of-war inmates. Among those prisoners was Newfoundland born John Ford. Camp Fukuoka was located on an island in the Harbour of Nagasaki, Japan.[1] As usual, the prisoners were awakened at 6:00 a.m. and were required to turn up for parade at 7:00 a.m. John Ford explained, "The first thing we did was to pick the bed lice and fleas off our bodies. Then we had to rub ourselves down just to get the circulation going, so we could work like slaves in the Mitsubishi Shipyard in Nagasaki. We were walking skeletons, the conditions were absolutely horrible." John Ford was 175 pounds when taken prisoner and on this day in 1945, he weighed only 93 pounds. He was serving with the Royal Air Force at Singapore when the Japanese had invaded and took him prisoner.

Photo Submitted
John Ford in British military uniform soon after arriving in Singapore.

In 1940, with the war raging in Europe, John Ford was in the fourth year of his employment as a machinist with the Reid Newfoundland Railway at Port aux Basques, Newfoundland. One day, a Magistrate John Pius Mulcahey arrived at Port aux Basques from St. John's with the Circuit Court and pinned a proclamation in the court house which attracted Ford's attention. It was a message from Prime Minister Winston Churchill appealing for volunteers to join the British mil-

---

1. There were two prison camps at Nagasaki named Camp Fukuoka. Camp Fukuoka #2 was on an island at the mouth of the Nagasaki Harbour. Camp Fukuoka #14 was about three miles from the Mitsubishi Shipyard.

itary in its war effort. In his message, Churchill made his famous statement, "I have nothing to offer you but blood, sweat, toil and tears." During my interview with John Ford on August 16, 2006, he showed his life experiences had not dulled his sense of humor. Referring to Churchill's pledge, Ford commented, "He gave all he promised and more besides."

With the adventure that brought him into the middle of one of the world's most horrible events now buried in the past, John Ford recalled how he was inspired to act

Photo Submitted
John Ford and future wife Margaret Payne on the day he left Port aux Basques to join the Royal Air Force in 1941.

by the Churchill proclamation. He decided then and there to take up the challenge, and he chose to join the Royal Air Force. Ford was twenty-one at the time. When he turned up at the recruiting station in the Church Lads Brigade Armory at St. John's, he learned that in order to join the RAF, he would have to go to London. To get to London, Ford had to join the Army. He did, and once in London, he transferred to the RAF.

It was May 1941 when Ford was assigned to the Thirty-six Torpedo Squadron and later transferred to Singapore, a place he had never heard of. He traveled to Singapore on the *Duchess of York* which carried 3500 soldiers and sailed in convoy stopping on the way at Freetown and Cape Town in South Africa, and Bombay, India before reaching his destination. Mr. Ford recalled his stay at Singapore:

The ten months I spent in Singapore were good ones. It was a different war at that time in the Far East than it was back home or in America. We had the best of everything, but it was too good to last.

Churchill had sent out officials to assess the ability of our forces in Singapore to defend against an attack by the Japanese. They found that the troops had insufficient arms to fend off any attack mounted by the enemy. The Japanese had a free hand in the Pacific after Pearl Harbour, and we knew they were going to attack. The British, led by commander-in-chief General Arthur Percival, capitulated on February 15, 1942, because they didn't want the Singapore citizens subjected to the same cruel treatment that the Japanese had earlier inflicted on the Chinese.

On the night of February 10, 1941, the Japanese came in from all sides to invade Singapore. At four o'clock in the morning, Ford took his bayonet and his 303 rifle and along with other members from his squadron, succeeded in escaping the invaders by boarding a tugboat. He recalled, "By this time the entire city was in flames, and the Japanese were shelling everything in the water. The captain of the tugboat told us that if we could man the tug, he would get us to Java."

Less than a month later, on March 8, 1942, the Japanese began dropping para-troops on Java. "A seaman on a ship leaving for Australia offered to take me on board, but I had sworn to serve as a soldier in the RAF and I could not break that oath. I had no choice but to stay with my fellow soldiers and share their fate." said Ford.

Ford and his comrades were taken prisoners by the Japanese. They were housed for days in shelters without food or any knowledge as to what plans the Japanese had in store for them. Villagers risked their lives by bringing food to them and shoving it in beneath the walls. They were then herded together for the long march from Keppel Harbour to Changhi Prison Camp in Singapore which the Japanese had taken from the British and used as their own.

The ordeal of the prisoners had just begun. Ford recalled the long march to the prison camp with its constant hardships and terror. Along the way there were signs that read, "White man go home. Asia for the Asians." It was a march he describes as "The March of Death":

> *It was very hot, and the pavement blistered our feet. The Japanese didn't want prisoners, we were nothing more than a bloody nuisance. Many men couldn't keep up, if they fell from exhaustion or the heat they never got up again. The Japanese guards killed them with their bayonets. They said shooting prisoners was a waste of bullets.*
>
> *Our captors were very cruel. During the long march to a prison camp, we saw the heads of former Chinese prisoners of war on fences. The guards would point out the heads and shout at us, saying that if we disobeyed them, the same thing would happen to us.*

At Changhi Camp we were divided into two groups to be shipped off to Japan. Mr. Ford began counting in Japanese to illustrate how the prisoners were split up. In this manner, he was separated from his buddy, Les Holman, who was from Bristol, England. When the Japanese officer doing the counting came to them, Ford was sent to one group, Holman to the other. It was the last time the two soldiers saw each other. Ford's group was destined to go to a labour camp in Japan to free up civilians to serve in the military, his friend's group was sent to another destination. The trip by boat to Japan was a hazardous one which Ford felt blessed to have survived. He said, "Over 17,000 prisoners of war were drowned or killed en route because the Americans and British torpedoed all ships not marked with the Red Cross flag. They had no idea that there were POWs on board." Ford learned later that the ship carrying his buddy had been torpedoed by the Americans.

On December 7, 1942, Ford arrived at Nagasaki. He was among the prisoners sent to Camp Fukuoka on an island in the middle of the harbour. For almost three years this would be his home.

At the prison camp, the Japanese assigned Ford the prisoner of war number '2207' and gave him a small rice can for his daily rations. Prisoner 2207 was assigned to work in the Mitsubishi Shipyard which was on the Island about one and a half miles from the prison camp. Ford was appointed as leader of a group of seven fellow prisoners working at the yard. The shipyard was controlled by the Japanese Navy. A Japanese Army escort would drop the prisoners at the yard each day, and they would be left under the control of the Navy who used civilians to manage these slave laborers.

Even though it has been more than sixty years since he was rescued from Camp Fukuoka, Ford has not forgotten how terrible life was there:

> *The conditions were atrocious. The Japanese were the roughest people that ever God created. It was slave labor. The prison camp was overcrowded with sixty prisoners crammed into one room. We were fed insect-infested rice and were given ragged clothing from Chinese prisoners. We had to be clean shaven and the Japanese guards showed delight in using sheep shears on us. We were allowed one bath every two weeks. Our captors did not supply us with soap, and forty men bathed at one time. I lost all sense of modesty, dignity and pride. This went on for three years. Prisoners suffered from dysentery, malaria, tuberculosis and diphtheria. We worked seven days a week and only got a work break when something good happened for the Japanese. When I arrived in Japan, I was 175 pounds and left weighing ninety-three pounds. I was a walking skeleton when I was finally freed. Medical attention was available, but if surgery was required, it was carried out without any anesthetics. Prisoners choose to suffer rather than ask for medical help.*

Conditions at the shipyard were even worse than at the prison camp. The shipyard was turning out one seven-thousand ton ship per month, and the men, already in deteriorating physical condition,

Carter/Fitzgerald Photography

Nagasaki Island where POW camp (extreme left) and Mitsubishi Shipyard (near centre) were located. Inserts: Newfoundland born John Ford, survivor of atomic bomb attack on Nagasaki.

were expected to keep up the pace. "If one person couldn't produce enough work, the entire group was punished by having its rations cut. However, what we did receive was shared and shared alike. We always tried to look out for each other," Ford explained.

John Ford worked on what was called the guillotine at the shipyard. This was a machine used to cut metal plates for the hull of the ship.

The first Atomic bomb was dropped on *Hiroshima* by the USAF B-29, remembered in history as the *Enola Gay,* on August 6, 1945. POWs at Camp Fukuoka were not told of that event. On August 9, 1945, a twist of fate caused a second bomber called *Bock's Car*[2], which carried the second A-bomb destined to be dropped on Japan,[3] to change its course and pick Nagasaki as its target. In the early morning, John Ford and fellow prisoners had no idea that the A-bomb even existed. Before noon they were wondering if the end of the world had come.

Ford was laboring under the intense summer heat at the Mitsubishi Shipyard when the bomb was dropped. He got a glimpse of the plane that dropped it as it turned to leave. His experience serving with the air-force enabled him to estimate the plane was flying at 33,000 feet. Decades later, when he befriended the pilot of that plane, Major Charles (Chuck) Sweeney, he learned that the plane was flying at 31,000 feet.[4]

At that time, he had no idea as to the identity of the plane. He explained :

> *Then the sun was completely blocked out, and I experienced the heat and blast of the explosion and the impact of it knocked me to the ground. The heat was unbearable. I saw people running and screaming with their flesh burning*

2. The plan was called after its previous commander, Captain Frederick Bock.
3. The actual destination of The Bock's Car is mentioned later in this story in a conversation between John Ford and the pilot of the aircraft which dropped the bomb.
4. In 1946 Major Charles Sweeney visited St. John's and stayed at the Newfoundland Hotel. He was interviewed by reporter Mike Critch, but at the time a veil of secrecy still covered the dropping of the A-bomb. He could only tell Critch that he was in Newfoundland on a special assignment which was classified.

Carter-Fitzgerald Photography
Author Jack Fitzgerald interviewing John Ford.

and their eyes popping out. We all thought the end of the world had come. It was unbelievable horror.

When the bomb was dropped, he was just seven kilometers from ground zero. He recalled seeing the mushroom cloud still rising and he added, "There was an intense heat everywhere and flesh was burning all around. Seventy thousand people were killed in an instant on that day." Almost one hundred of Ford's comrades at Camp Fukuoka had been severely burned.

While pandemonium reigned, Ford's captors were confused and not sure what to do. Near their work site, the Japanese had constructed shelters which, according to Ford, they had planned to use to gas prisoners if the Americans launched an invasion of Japan. The POWs were gathered and herded into these shelters where they remained for more than an hour. Then the prison guards arrived and took them back to Camp Fukuoka. Ford recalled that from this point on, they knew that something had changed in the war because their captors began to treat them better. The commanding officer told them they would have a good meal that night. For the first time since being imprisoned they had food other than rice. The good meal consisted of a half can of beef per man, and there was some Chinese green tea.

The next day a USAF plane flew over the camp, but the Japanese still had not told the prisoners about what had happened. Ford enlisted the support of other inmates in taking their blankets and spelling out the word "News" on the grounds of the prison camp. The aircraft flew over a second time and understood the message. The pilot returned later and dropped food along with printed messages stating that the war was over.

A prized possession of Ford which he took with him to his home in Newfoundland in 1945 and, which he treasures to this day, is one of the silk pillow slips the Japanese issued to each prisoner upon arrival at the POW camp. These were empty when given, and

Carter/Fitzgerald Photography

Artifact from Nagasaki bombing.

the Japanese left it to the prisoners to use whatever they could find to fill them. After the bombing of Nagasaki, and the first arrival of USAF planes over Camp Fukuoka, this pillow slip took on a very special significance to Ford. When the USAF bomber flew over the camp and dropped food, R. A. Hemmings, a friend and fellow prisoner with Ford, used several colored pencils in his possession to sketch a picture of the American plane flying over the camp, with details that identified the Squadron, the package dropping from the plane, and a Japanese guard painting POW on the roof of the prison dormitory where Ford was held. When it was completed, Hemmings signed it and gave it to his friend John Ford. Several years ago, Ford ran into a mutual friend of his and Hemmings, and when told that Hemmings was still alive, Ford asked the friend to tell him, "I still have the pillow-slip." Apart from a little soiling over the years, mostly accumulated from being used in the POW camp, this unique drawing — and tangible connection with a historic world event — remains in remarkably good shape. Ford has other mementoes of his service in the Far East, including Chinese money, hotel checks, pictures of Singapore, including a gruesome photograph showing the recovery of a full goat from the stomach of a large boa constrictor.

A short time after the food drop by the USAF Bomber, American troops arrived at the Camp, and the sick and injured were the first to be evacuated. The prisoners went through the delousing process before heading home. They traveled from Nagasaki on the aircraft carrier *U.S. Chenango* to Okinawa where they were housed overnight in canvas tents. The following morning John Ford was among the soldiers taken on a B24 bomber to Manila where they were placed on a special diet. On September 13, 1945, Ford left Manila for Canada on the aircraft carrier the *US Implacable*. He arrived in Vancouver on October 24, and the following day the Vancouver Sun carried a front page story with pictures of Ford and several other soldiers, returning home from Japanese prison camps.

On November 2, 1945, after Ford had returned to Newfoundland, the *Evening Telegram* at St. John's reported:

*Aircraftsman Ford is still suffering from the effects of
the brutal treatment he received at the hands of the
Japanese and can only take liquid food. En route to his
home at Port aux Basques, he paid a brief visit to his sister,
Mrs. Angus Bowdridge at Halifax.*

Sometime later, a reporter asked how he felt in the days following the *A-Bomb* attack, Ford replied:

*At that time, I had suffered so much, I wouldn't have
cared if they had dropped ten bombs. If the Americans had
decided to invade by foot instead of using the bomb, we
would have all been killed anyway. The Japanese had
planned to kill all prisoners if the Americans invaded.*[5]

An interesting statistic for those who were prisoners of the
Japanese was that the mortality rate in the Japanese camps was thirty-five per cent while in the German prison camps it was just five
percent. Ford explained that this was due, in part, to the fact the
Japanese had refused to sign the terms of the Geneva Convention.

John Ford was home only a week when he received orders
from the RAF to return to England by December 17. This man
who had given so much in the service of his country was required
to spend another Christmas away from home. He made his way
through Halifax to New York City where he boarded the *Queen
Elizabeth Two* which took him to South Hampton, England. When
he reported for duty, the officer in charge viewed his file and wondered aloud what he was doing back in England.

His stay in England was short, and during July 1946 John Ford
retired from the Royal Air Force. He returned to Newfoundland
and resumed his job with the Newfoundland Railway where he
worked his way up to management level, retiring in 1976.

Since the end of the war, Ford has had many conversations
with Major Sweeney. He was told that the actual target for bomb-

5. The commanding officer at Camp Fukuoka #2 was tried for war crimes and sentenced to
eight years imprisonment.

ing on August 9 was a city called Kokura. By August 6, 1945, the Americans had narrowed down the sites under consideration as targets for the A-bomb to three cities. First was Hiroshima, where there were no POW camps, although fourteen recently captured USAF soldiers were being held for interrogation inside of Hiroshima Castle. The second target choice was Kokura, which had military and munitions targets, and thirdly was Nagasaki.

When Sweeney arrived at Kokura it was clouded over and he couldn't see his target. He then changed his destination to Nagasaki where, Ford recalls, he dropped the Atomic bomb at exactly 11:02 a.m. Sweeney told Ford that as he flew over Nagasaki, he was well aware that there was a POW camp there, but explained that he had his orders. Sweeney choose to drop the Atomic bomb in the northwestern section of Nagasaki partly to minimize its affect on the POW camps.[6] Unlike the Atomic bomb dropped on Hiroshima which was a uranium bomb, the one dropped on Nagasaki was a more powerful plutonium bomb. It caused less damage than the Hiroshima bombing because of the difference in the Nagasaki terrain. Regardless, its effect was devastating.

Another interesting anecdote Sweeney told Ford was that they took off from Tinian Isle in the South Pacific in a half million dollar plane that carried a two billion dollar bomb. At the time of take off, there were problems with the fueling of the plane. Sweeney was told it would take another six hours to correct it. Sweeney decided to take off anyway rather than deviate from his schedule. After dropping the bomb, *Bock's Car* turned and headed back. Because he did not have access to his full load of fuel, he just managed to reach Okinawa where he made a safe landing.[7]

Ford continues to treasure several keepsakes from his wartime service. While a prisoner in Japan, he was allowed to send only four very short messages home. These were written in his own

6. *Enola Gay*, Gordon Thomas and Max Morgan Witts, Simon and Shuster Publishing, New York, 1976.
7. When *Bock's Car* was fueled, access to one of the fuel tanks was blocked and Sweeney had decided to proceed on his mission rather than disrupt his schedule. This created the problem of getting back safely.

handwriting and then typed onto post cards by a Japanese soldier. He had all four laminated to preserve them.

At age 87, John Ford has a phenomenal memory. Not only does he recall the intricate details of his ordeal in the Far East and his encounter with the A-bomb, but he kept a record of information which years later proved vital in dealing with the bureaucratic red tape that surrounded veterans' programs which were developed to help survivors of Japanese POW camps.

Several years ago, W.J. Prosser, a fellow prisoner from Camp Fukuoka, passed away and his widow had applied for a lump sum payment available to the Japanese POWs. The British Veteran Affairs Department refused the application because there were others with the same name, and Veterans Affairs required his service number to prove he had been at Camp Fukuoka. The family made every effort to convince authorities of the validity of its claim, but without his service number the effort was useless. Eventually, a friend of the family suggested they contact John Ford and added that if anyone could confirm that Prosser had been at the Japanese prison camp, it would be Ford.

Ford received a call from Prosser's son, who, after identifying himself, asked if Ford remembered a fellow prisoner in Japan named W. Prosser. "Remember him, I can give you his service number as well as the prisoner-of-war number given to him by the Japanese," answered John Ford.

"Well, that is why I am calling, my mother really needs that number," said the caller as he outlined the problem she was experiencing.

Bob Rumsey Photo
John Ford at home in St. John's, 2006.

"Just a minute and I'll get it for you," said Ford.

He referred to his collection of papers and removed a list of all his friends at Camp Fukuoka. From the list he gave the caller the information requested. Prosser's Royal Air Force number was *542587* and he had served with the 36 Squadron of the RAF. The number assigned to him by the Japanese was number *2235*. Mrs. Prosser had her lump sum payment from the British Government soon after.

A very special memento of his horrific experiences in Japan was a letter from the King of England which acknowledged John Ford's Japanese experience. It read:

The Queen and I bid you a very warm welcome home. Through all the great trials and suffering which you have undergone at the hands of the Japanese you and your comrades have been constantly in our thoughts. We know from the accounts we have already received how heavy the sufferings have been. We know also that these have been endured by you with highest courage. We mourn with you the death of so many of your gallant comrades. With all our hearts, we hope that your return from captivity will bring you and your family a full measure of happiness which you may long enjoy together.

It was signed by King George V and has three war stamps alongside the signature.

Today, John Ford hopes that the A-bomb will never have to be used again. He said, "I saw the damage, pain and destruction caused by the A-bomb, and I never want to hear tell of it being dropped again. There's enough harm in this world today."

In October 1946, Ford married Margaret Payne and they had one son Robert. Doctors who examined him after he returned from Japan in 1945 predicted he would not live past the age of forty. Since that time he has suffered and recovered from four skin cancers due to exposure to radiation from the bomb. Today John Ford is eighty-seven years old. He was born on March 25, 1919.

In 2002, he was featured in a CBC documentary which took him back to Nagasaki for the first time since the end of the war. He met with several Japanese government officials and visited the site of the former Camp Fukuoka as well as the A-bomb Museum. He described his reaction:

> *Nagasaki is a very different place today. The hardship is gone, but the memories are still there. I can forgive, but I can't forget and I don't want to forget, because we must never allow history to repeat itself. Anyone who doesn't want peace has no concept or understanding of human life. I gave four of the best years of my life for freedom, and I hope the world is a better place for it. However, many men gave their lives.*

The Mayor of Nagasaki told Ford that he was eligible to come to Japan and be treated at Japanese expense for any illness resulting from the radiation generated by the bomb, but Ford declined saying that he had good medical coverage in Canada.

In 2005, Ford, his wife and son Robert were flown to Ottawa where they attended the memorial services marking the 60th anniversary of the ending of World War Two. Ford feels that people don't seem to realize the losses suffered in the Far East by the Allies. Of the 5000 POWs there, 1740 did not return.

Another twist in the story of John Ford is that twenty years after the bombing of Hiroshima, the flight engineer on the *Enola Gay*, the name given by its crew to the USAF-B29 bomber that dropped the A-bomb on Hiroshima, was living at Harmon Air Force Base, Stephenville, just miles from where Ford was born and worked after the war.

The bombing of Hiroshima and Nagasaki brought an end to World War II, but it ignited a controversy that may never be settled. It centered around the question, "Was the Atomic Bomb attack necessary?"

The mathematical formula of Albert Einstein was used by scientists in the United States to build the A-bomb. The invention changed civilization forever.

In an interview with the *Evening Telegram* in 1962, Staff
Sergeant Wyatt Duzenbury said that he felt no regret and no
remorse for his part in the bombing. Duzenbury was described as
a man dedicated to his life in the air force. He was never one to
boast about his role in history, and when asked about it, brushed it
off as being part of his duty as a soldier.
He told the *Telegram*:

> As a soldier, we were directed to a mission and we did
> it. Under the same circumstances I would have no com-
> punction in doing the same again. There was only one
> beach-head remaining in the war and that was the island
> shores of Japan itself. We knew that such an attack on
> Japan would cost an inestimable number of civilian and
> military casualties. However, the dropping of the A-bomb
> was in the general interest of all.

Like Duzenbury, John Ford displayed the same loyalty and
dedication to his role in the military when he declined the opportunity to escape the Japanese at Java in favor of remaining to share
the same fate as his comrades in the RAF.

Chapter 2

The Arctic - The Disaster Newfoundland Wanted Forgotten!

The Arctic Disaster – A Newfoundland Scandal

During the summer of 1854, William Brown, part-owner of the Collins Shipping Line, one of the world's largest passenger-mail steamship services, stopped at the shop of a gypsy fortune teller in London, England, to have his palm read. It was a day of recreation for Mr. Brown and the idea of having his future told amused him. Part way through the session, the gypsy's facial expression contorted as she grasped Brown's wrist tightly and said, "You will die in a horrible shipwreck." Mr. Brown sought more detailed information, but the gypsy ended the session abruptly with the comment, "I have nothing more to tell you."

On September 20, 1854, when Brown stepped onto the deck of the *Arctic,* a Collins Liner, to begin his cross-Atlantic trip to his home in New York, he suddenly froze as he recalled the gypsy's warning. He quickly dispelled these thoughts as mere superstition and went over to greet Captain James Luce, the ship's captain and a long-time friend. A week later William Brown's body was float-ing in the Atlantic waters off Cape Race, Newfoundland, and the *Arctic* lay on the bottom of the ocean.

Following the sinking of the *Titanic* in 1912, journalists across North America sought out stories to parallel the *Titanic* tragedy. One of those which attracted much attention was the sinking of the *Arctic* fifty miles off Cape Race, south of St. John's in 1854.

The 3000-ton vessel carried a total of 383 persons of whom 233 were passengers and 150 were crewmembers. Among the passen-gers were the wife and two children of the general manager of the Collins Line. Like the *Titanic,* the *Arctic* failed to carry enough lifeboats to evacuate all on board, even though the vessel carried the minimum number of lifeboats required by law.

The story of the *Arctic* stands out in the history of shipwrecks, not only for the great loss of life, but for the disgraceful conduct of some of the crew in rushing to abandon the sinking ship and leav-ing women and children on board to face certain death. Equally disgraceful was the failure of the Newfoundland Government and the American Consul in St. John's to initiate an immediate rescue effort. The lack of leadership for almost a week after the shipwreck will always remain a source of shame for Newfoundland. No wonder, for decades afterwards, many in Newfoundland wanted to forget the *Arctic* disaster.

The *Arctic* — a world-famous paddle steamer — was the *Titanic* of its day. Reverend John Steven Carl Abbott, who crossed the Atlantic in 1852 on the *Arctic,* wrote in Harper's Magazine, "Never did there float upon the ocean a more magnificent palace." The vessel measured 284 feet on deck, 277.3 feet on keel and 45.8 feet wide across the main deck. The width expanded to seventy-two feet in the area where the paddle-boxes on the side of the ship were located.

At this time in history, when shipping was moving from sail to steam engine, the great American Collins Shipping Line[1] was in strong competition with the British Cunard Shipping Line on the trans-Atlantic passenger service. Both the Collins Line and the Cunard Line received very large subsidies from their respective governments to carry mail across the Atlantic. In the case of the Collins Line that subsidy was $33,000 per round trip. The Collins Liners were faster and more luxurious that the Cunard vessels and they had succeeded in getting the U.S. mail contracts based on their commitment to provide the fastest cross-Atlantic service.

On September 13, 1854, the *Arctic,* under the command of forty-nine-year-old Captain James C. Luce, sailed into Liverpool Harbour. Captain Luce brought along his handicapped twelve-year-old son who needed assistance in walking. Both the Captain and his wife had felt that the trip would do much to lift the spirits of the boy and perhaps even improve his health.

At noon, September 20, the *Arctic* departed from Liverpool for New York. All passenger tickets had been sold and some wishing to purchase tickets had to be turned away. Among the passengers were several wealthy New York residents, a French Duke going to Washington to take up a diplomatic post with the French Embassy, a courier named George Burns of Philadelphia, who was carrying dispatches for U.S. President James Buchanan, and the wife of the

---

1. The legal name for the Collins' Line was the New York and Liverpool U.S. Mail Steamship Company, which was incorporated on November 1, 1847.

Collins Line general manager and part owner, Mrs. Edward Collins and their two children, nineteen-year-old Mary Anne, and fifteen-year-old Henry.

Among those unable to get passage was a group of nuns who were traveling to serve in a convent-school in California. The eighteen nuns were disappointed when told they had to wait for the next ship leaving Liverpool for the U.S. Little did they know what a blessing that delay would become for them.

As the *Arctic* steamed across the Grand Banks of Newfoundland on Wednesday, September 27, about fifty miles from Cape Race, Captain Luce was pleased with his progress. He was now only three days from New York. The early morning fog had improved very little. It continued with intermittent intervals of visibility which at times enabled officers of the *Arctic* to see one or two miles ahead. Regardless of the visibility, Captain Luce gave no thought to reducing speed because the vessel was making record time. However, at least one passenger, a Scotsman, was anxious about the situation. The fact that the ship had no alarm bells or steam whistle to warn of danger added to his anxiety.

At 12:15 a.m., at longitude 46 degrees 45' north by 52 degrees 60' west, a lookout shouted, "There's a steamer ahead." This was followed seconds later by a deck officer's command, "Hard a-starboard," then "Stop her!" The ship's annunciator was used to signal the order to stop and change direction.[2] The sudden change in the ship's course caused Captain Luce to drop what he was doing and rush to the deck. He arrived there just as a dark barque-rigged steamer emerged out of the fog on a collision course with the *Arctic*.

The dark ship emerging out of the fog was the 250-ton French steamer and sailing ship, the *Vesta* that had just left St. Pierre carrying 150 fishermen home to France for the winter. It had been built at Nantes, France in 1853 for the firm Hernoux et Compagnie of Dieppe, France, and carried a crew of fifteen. The *Vesta*'s 60 hp engine needed the help of the vessel's sails to gain speed during its Atlantic crossing.

2. An Annunciator was an in-house bell communication system used to communicate within a ship, building or house.

Designed to carry cargo and 150 passengers with limited space, the *Vesta* measured 152' L, 20.3' W and was 10.4' in depth. By the time she came into view of the *Arctic*, both vessels were traveling at twelve knots, which was the top speed of the era. The *Vesta* and *Arctic* came into view of each other at the same time and both initiated actions to avoid a collision. It was too late. There was not enough distance between the two for maneuvering and the fate of almost six hundred people was sealed.

Although the impact of the collision was hardly noticed on the *Arctic*, it was significantly felt on the *Vesta*. The *Vesta*'s passengers rushed to the deck in confusion and were convinced by what they saw that their ship was going to sink. Two lifeboats were launched in hopes of getting to the *Arctic*, which at first appeared not to have suffered any serious damage. During the escape effort one of the lifeboats capsized and the second was ordered by the vessel's captain to remain by the ship.

At first, The *Arctic*'s captain felt his ship would survive the collision, and sent Robert J. Gourley, his first mate, along with eight of his crew, to offer assistance to the *Vesta*. Soon after these men left the ship, Captain Luce was made aware that the *Arctic* had been seriously damaged below the waterline. The collision had left the *Arctic* with a five-foot-wide hole in its side beneath the waterline. Some crewmen, led by the ship's carpenter, made an unsuccessful attempt to cover the hole with sail canvas.

While pandemonium reigned on deck, Captain Luce thought it necessary to take a brief moment to reassure his son. One of the most touching moments of the tragedy occurred when young "Willie" Luce, propped up on his pillows, told his father, "Don't mind me father. Go back on deck, you're wanted there to take care of the ship." The *Arctic* circled the *Vesta* twice while Captain Luce assessed the damage. Those on the *Vesta* seeing one of the *Arctic*'s lifeboats approaching them, and the *Arctic* circling, were convinced that they were going to be rescued. The fog quickly covered the area and when it lifted, Captain Alphonse Duchesne, his crew and passengers on the *Vesta* were astounded to watch the *Arctic* sail away instead of staying at the scene to assist them.

The Captain and crew of the *Vesta* turned their attention to keeping their vessel afloat, while Captain Luce concluded that the only chance to save the *Arctic* was to move full speed towards the Newfoundland coast, before water pouring into the ship from the damaged section below the waterline filled and sank her. He had no time to communicate his intentions to those on the *Vesta*. This decision would later cause much confusion and bad feelings towards *Arctic* survivors as they arrived at St. John's.

During its move from the accident site, the *Arctic*'s paddle crushed a *Vesta* lifeboat carrying eight men. Only one man survived. A young German passenger on the *Arctic* tossed him a rope and succeeded in pulling him to temporary safety. About forty miles from Cape Race, the sea had flooded the engine rooms and shut down the engines. The *Arctic* slowed to a complete stop and despite the efforts of Captain Luce and a few loyal crewmen, some of the crew disregarded the principle of 'women and children first,' and took control of some lifeboats for themselves. There was a great deal of confusion and panic as others attempted to escape the sinking vessel. Due to the inadequate number of lifeboats on the *Arctic,* most on board were unable to escape and tragically went down with the ship.

Two of the *Arctic*'s lifeboats, carrying a total of forty-five crew and passengers, met as they distanced themselves from the damaged vessel. A quick discussion took place between both groups and a joint decision was made to make Second Mate William Baalham their captain and allow him to direct their efforts to row safely to the Newfoundland coast. A suggestion that they return to the shipwreck scene to rescue more survivors was quickly dashed by those who thought that people struggling to get out of the water might cause the lifeboats to tip over or sink. They also felt there was a great danger in being close when the *Arctic* finally tipped and submerged into the ocean, perhaps dragging those nearby with them.

After rowing forty-two hours and enduring cold, dampness and hunger, Baalham's lifeboats came within view of Cappahayden (Broad Cove in the nineteenth century) at about 4:00 a.m. on

Friday, September 29. Baalham took time to size up the coastline and then selected an area on Cappahayden beach most suitable for an easy landing. His decision proved to be a sound one and the two lifeboats easily landed at the site.

Once safely on land, the survivors bowed their heads and offered up a prayer of thanksgiving for their deliverance. One survivor praised Baalham's skill and leadership in bringing them to safety.

While preparing to leave the beach, they heard a dog barking, which led them to the house of Jack Fleming near the top of a crest overlooking the beach. Fleming, a fisherman, occupied the small cabin with his son, Joseph.

He had little in the way of supplies but what he had he shared willingly. There was plenty of fresh water, which was more than welcomed by the survivors, and then there was 'hard tack' or 'biscuit' used by those who went to sea because it lasted a long while without going bad. As meager as the rations were, they were more than the survivors had eaten in two days.

Fleming briefed the survivors on the route to St. John's and the communities they would pass through on the journey. The first of these would be Renews. Fleming had sent his son ahead to Renews to advise them that shipwreck survivors were on the way. The good people there moved quickly to welcome them and offer assistance.

Jack Fleming became known for decades after for his stories about the terrible *Arctic* disaster and the survivors who made it to Cappahayden.

Two of the survivors, injured during the mad rush to take control of the lifeboats while evacuating the *Arctic,* were left behind in Fleming's care. Baalham then led the remainder of the group on the four-mile trek to Renews. By the time they arrived, the people there were waiting to welcome them into their homes. Food, medicines, warm clothing and bedding were supplied to each of them.

Baalham was determined to get back to the shipwreck scene as quickly as possible. Along with the *Arctic*'s purser John Geib, they hired two small fishing schooners, one to return to the *Arctic* to search for survivors and the other to take the remaining survivors to St. John's, about fifty miles east of Renews.

City of St. John's Archives

Water Street in St. John's in the nineteenth century.

Heavy winds struck the area and the schooner carrying the survivors to St. John's was forced to take shelter at Ferryland. Once
more Newfoundlanders treated them kindly, and their stay in the
community was made as comfortable as possible. Many were
housed in private homes while the crew was given shelter at the
Ferryland Court House. The strong winds sweeping the shore continued throughout the weekend.

A small band of six of the survivors chose not to wait for the
weather to improve, and they set out on foot towards St. John's,
where they arrived around 5:30 p.m. on Monday, October 2. This
first group of *Arctic* survivors was amazed to learn that the *Vesta*
had survived. It had made it safely to St. John's with all but a dozen
of its crew and passengers, who had died during escape efforts soon
after the collision.

Before leaving Ferryland, Geib, unaware of the *Vesta*'s arrival
in St. John's, sent a message to the U.S. Consul at St. John's with
the request that it be forwarded onto the Collins Office in New
York. The *Vesta*'s damage appeared to be so serious that the Arctic
survivors were convinced it could not have stayed afloat any more
than a half hour. In his message to St. John's, Geib reported with

certainty that the *Vesta* had gone down. In addition to having mistakenly reported that the *Vesta* had gone down at sea, Geib reported that the family of the general manager of the Collins Line had made it to his (Geib's) lifeboat but were washed overboard and drowned. Later events show that this was not correct.

It is important to record the efforts of Captain Alphonse Duchesne to make it to St. John's, a mere five hours away. He first calmed down passengers and crew who were visibly upset by what appeared to be the *Arctic*'s callous abandonment of them.

This was followed by an assessment of the damage received by the *Vesta* in the collision and a plan of survival. The Author of *Rivalry on the Atlantic*, Commander W. Mack Angus, U.S.N. wrote in his book:

> *It appears that after quelling the initial panic on the* Vesta, *Captain Duchesne found that the forward collision bulkhead was holding in spite of the almost compete loss of the forward ten feet of the ship. He therefore lightened the bow by cutting down and throwing overboard the foremast, stiffened the bulkhead with such bracing and temporary shoring as could be improvised, and made for St. John's under reduced speed.*

Duchesne felt that his ship had to be further lightened to survive. He ordered that the barrels of oil and fish representing the fishermen's hard work and earnings for the fishing season be jettisoned into the Atlantic before the *Vesta* would set out for St. John's. His efforts paid off and the ship made it to the safety of St. John's Harbour just as a heavy windstorm was striking. Had that storm hit earlier it is doubtful that the *Vesta* would have survived. The *Vesta*, with 200 people on board, had lost only thirteen in the disaster. One was killed in the collision, others died after jumping into the sea and the *Arctic* crushed the remainder.

Fortunately, the *Vesta* had been better built to survive at sea than the large, more expensive, luxury-liner *Arctic*. Her biggest advantage over the *Arctic* was the safety system that involved three watertight bulkheads, which divided her holds and engine room into separate compartments.

In his book *Women and Children Last, The loss of the Steamship Arctic*, Author Alexander Crosby Brown noted:

> *This was a safety system of sufficient antiquity to have been described to the western world by Marco Polo upon his return from his classic voyage to the Orient, but considered in the 1850s of no particularly striking consequence. By contrast, the* Arctic *though hailed as the latest word in ship construction, was open from stem to stern as a canoe.*
>
> *The wood of the* Arctic *was reinforced with iron rods while the* Vesta*'s hull was built of seven-millimeter thick iron plates in her bottom. Despite not having sufficient numbers of lifeboats for the number of passengers and crew on the* Arctic, *the vessel was equipped with the number of lifeboats required by law and these were the latest and best of available equipment. The U.S. Federal Government steamboat law of April 30, 1852 required all passenger vessels to carry at least one metal lifeboat. The* Arctic*'s lifeboats were made of corrugated galvanized iron. The* Arctic *also carried an ample supply of life preservers and a metal "life car" for bringing passengers ashore on a beach.*

Touissant's Hotel on Water Street[3] opened its doors to *Vesta* survivors and assisted those who could not be accommodated in finding shelter at other hotels and lodging houses in the city. *The Public Ledger,* a St. John's newspaper, praised the actions of Captain Alphonse Duchesne in keeping his damaged vessel afloat and making it to St. John's. It noted, "Nothing but the most indomitable energy, unwavering perseverance, and the most superior seamanship could have succeeded in bringing the *Vesta* to port."

The first word of the *Arctic* disaster was received in St. John's by American Consul William Henry Newman on Saturday after-

---

3. Touissant's was located where the King George V Building is now located on the eastern end of Water Street.

noon from John Geib, Purser on board the *Arctic*. At the time John Geib sent his message to St. John's, he was not aware that the *Vesta* had survived. His letter reflected this belief:

> *Messrs. E.K. Collins & Co., New York*
>   *On Wednesday, 27th instant at 12 o'clock, the* Arctic *came into collision with a screw steamer (name unknown) in a dense fog, 55 miles south-east of Cape Race, which resulted in the destruction of both vessels, the latter in 30 minutes carrying down all on board. In an hour and a half from the time of collision the engines of the* Arctic *ceased working on account of the fires being extinguished and the passengers and crew took to the boats, as far as able. The number of persons that arrived here in safety in two boats, one of which I had charge of, was 45 — 14 passengers and 31 crew. A number of persons were lost by the swamping of one of the boats, in which it is painful for me to say, were Mr. and Mrs. Collins and their daughter Mary Anne. We landed at a place called Renews in Newfoundland and are now on our way to St. John's — distant about 50 miles, where I send this communication by Express to the American Consul to forward to Halifax. I have chartered a schooner, which sailed this morning with a fair wind, under command of Mr. Baalham, the second officer, which will probably arrive at the scene of the disaster at 12 o'clock tonight, 29th, in search of the other boats out. Annexed I send a list of passengers and crew saved in the two boats with me.*
>   *Signed – John Geib, Purser*

Geib had incorrectly reported that the Collins family (wife and children of E.K. Collins, general manager and part owner of the Collins Lines) made it off the ship in a lifeboat but the boat was swamped and they were all drowned. Testimony given at the enquiry held later showed that Mrs. Collins and her two children remained on the *Arctic* to the last.

Ferryland, 29th Sept., 1854
W.H. Newman, Esq., American Consul.
Dear Sir,
    Enclosed I send you an important telegraphic commu-
nication for Messrs. E.K. Collins & Co., New York, inform-
ing them of the loss of the steamer Arctic, which I will
thank you to have forwarded to Halifax for transmission by
the earliest opportunity from St. John's. I am now on my
way to your place with 14 passengers and 31 of the crew of
the ill-fated steamer, who were saved in two small boats
belonging to the ship after spending two days and two
nights on the deep. We arrived at 4 o'clock this morning at
a place called Broad Cove⁴, and are waiting for a fair wind
to take us to St. John's.

B John Geib, Purser

Vesta survivors who were sheltered at St. John's began telling
outrageous stories of the *Arctic* abandoning them and sailing away
from the crash scene without offering help. A few days later when
the *Arctic* survivors began trickling into St. John's, they were not
given the same warm welcome and support that had been so generously given along the Southern Shore of the Avalon Peninsula.

    While the survivors of the *Arctic* fought for life just five hours
from St. John's, the response to news of the tragedy in the capital
city was outrageous. Those in a position to initiate an immediate
response did nothing. Although the Governor, Prime Minister,
American Consul, and Steam Ship Manager all lived within a one-
mile radius of each other, they never came together in one unified
meeting to develop a rescue strategy. Instead, there was a spectacle like something out of a Buster Keaton movie, with key players
resting on Sunday, bumping into each other on St. John's streets
over the next days, exchanging suggestions on what should be done
then running off in all directions, all this while precious hours were
passing, and men, women and children were struggling to survive
not far from the capital city.

4. Broad Cove was renamed Cappahayden in the early 20th century.

Instead of sparking an all-out organized search for survivors, there was little sense of urgency, and the matter was tossed back and forth among those who had it in their power to respond immediately.

The first person to react was Bishop Edward Feild, Anglican Bishop of Newfoundland. Bishop Feild, upon hearing of the tragedy, rushed to the Commercial Chambers in downtown St. John's where some of the prominent merchants of St. John's were relaxing and discussing the news of the day. Feild told them that his yacht the *Hawk* was ready to go immediately to search for survivors. The merchants threw cold water on the idea, asking who would pay the expenses. They indicated they would not be sending ships to participate in any search. Bishop Feild left the chambers and sought out Prime Minister Little and Governor Ker Baillie Hamilton.

The response by the authorities and merchants of St. John's to news of the *Arctic* disaster will remain a black mark on Newfoundland's otherwise outstanding record in coming to the aid of fellow human beings involved in tragedy in its waters. This unconscionable response was reflected in the conduct of those who could have acted immediately to launch a comprehensive rescue effort, but did not.

Although the American Consul was informed of the tragedy on the afternoon of Saturday, September 30, and initiated efforts to relay this information to the United States and to initiate a search, Prime Minister P.F. Little was not moved to action until Monday, October 2. In a letter to local newspapers on October 7, 1854, he explained:

> *Between 2 and 3 o'clock, p.m. a gentleman called on me, stating that no steps had been taken by anybody in St. John's to rescue such of her surviving passengers and crew as had not reached the land, and were then supposed to be at the mercy of the waves not far from our coast. I immediately waited on Mr. Newman, the American Consul, in company with my informant, and inquired from him what measures he had taken, and if he had solicited the*

Governor's assistance to save the unfortunate survivors. He replied that he had sent off a letter to a vessel bound to Boston, to be delivered at some intermediate port, for the purpose of telegraphing the news of the disaster to New York, but that she had sailed; that, Dr. Feild had kindly offered his yacht, which he was about to fit out and dispatch in search of the Arctic *and her boats; that he had been at the Commercial Room, where cold water was thrown on his efforts by some of the mercantile gentlemen present, who asked him "Who was going to guarantee the expenses of sending out vessels?" and that he was going to the Governor.*

Prime Minister Little's letter drew this angry response from the Editor of the *Newfoundlander* on October 9:

The question will inevitably suggest itself to every rational inquirer, why information which reached the hands of the American Consul at 7 o'clock on Saturday evening was not sufficiently "certain" to have impelled men in the name of a Government to immediate action for the rescue of human life. Will they inform the American or British people, what they did on Saturday evening on receipt of this "not certain" intelligence? And why sailing craft — abundant in port — were not dispatched at least by daylight next day in quest of the Arctic's *victims? Then they conveniently ignore the intervening Sunday and tell us of a communication of the Government to Mr. Newman, on Monday morning — this turning out to have been on Monday between 2 and 3 o'clock when Mr. Little was in conversation with the Consul. But even if this "morning" statement were not a proven falsehood, what were they about all Sunday. Was the best of days a dics non in the estimation of this Christian Government, while the lives of 350 fellow-beings hung upon the thread of an immediate deliverance?*

Meanwhile, while Prime Minister Little was meeting with the American Consul on Monday, he encouraged the Consul to go see Governor Ker Baillie Hamilton as soon as possible. The Prime Minister said:

> *Steam vessels should be sent to the calamity without delay, and distinctly authorized him to inform his Excellency that I should undertake on behalf of the majority of the House of Assembly, to indemnify him for any outlay that would be necessary in the adoption of every available means to rescue the lives of the survivors. While we were conversing, a letter was received by him from the Secretary's Office tendering the cooperation of the Governor in any efforts that he might dream expedient to adopt under the circumstances.*[5]

Following his meeting with Newman, Prime Minister Little obtained support from a majority of members of the House of Assembly who signed an indemnity to the Governor to cover the costs the American Consul would need to incur immediately in obtaining a vessel or vessels to go to the rescue of survivors. According to the Prime Minister, while he was out that night the American Consul accompanied by Mr. Joseph Crowdy of the Secretary's Office had called at the Prime Minister's house. When the PM learned of this visit, he went to see the Consul but he was not at home. The PM did not make contact with the Consul again until noon the next day. The two men, who were in a position of sending aid to the shipwreck scene, encountered each other while walking on a downtown street. Still, no suggestion had been made of a joint meeting with the Governor of all parties in a position to mount an organized rescue effort.

The Consul informed him that he could not come to an agreement with Chandler White, Vice-President of the New York, Newfoundland and London Telegraph Company, over the hiring of the *Victoria*, which was owned by the Telegraph Company. The

5. The *Newfoundlander*, St. John's, Nl. Monday October 9, 1854.

dispute was over the mode of payment. The *Victoria* was operating out of St. John's laying the western end of the Atlantic Cable. She was fully equipped for sea and ready to sail. Chandler White, after listening carefully to Newman outline the plight of the *Arctic* shocked the American Consul by, without hesitation, demanding $500 a day for use of the *Victoria* in a rescue effort.

Newman had felt this was "robbery" and well beyond what he could authorize. He communicated the situation to the American Secretary of State, William L. Marry, in Washington. Just weeks before the tragedy Roman Catholic Bishop J.T. Mullock had publicly praised Chandler White for his philanthropy in giving a generous donation to the Roman Catholic Church.

Little offered to meet with White to make sure he understood the commitment the Government had made to the American Consul. By this time the American Consul had little faith that any more survivors could be found. He viewed all efforts at this point as, "keeping up appearances." The Prime Minister said he did not agree and had convinced White to accept an order on the local Government payable in thirty days for the use of the *Victoria* at the rate agreed to by Mr. Newman.

When informed by the Prime Minister of White's acceptance of a deal, Newman responded that it was too late. He said he had obtained the services of the mail ship *Merlin*. Despite this turn of events, there was still no sense of urgency. On Tuesday evening, seventy-two hours after news of the disaster had reached St. John's, the agents of the *Merlin,* the only steamer ready to respond, posted a notice at the Post Office that the mails should be closed at the usual time, as it was not their intention to send off the steamer sooner, "unless" commanded to do so by the Governor.

The failure to mount a rescue effort continued and on Wednesday morning, E. Shea, MHA, St. Mary's and Placentia, volunteered to meet with the Governor and present him with the letter of indemnity the Prime Minister had prepared two days earlier.

On Wednesday morning, four days after learning of the *Arctic* disaster, the politicians were still arguing over who would pay and, as a consequence, they had not initiated any rescue effort. The

American Consul contacted the Prime Minister on Wednesday morning to find out why the *Victoria* was getting up her steam. He was anxious to know where she was going, and told the Prime Minister that he had been 'humbugged' by the agents of the *Merlin*, " ...who did not intend sending her away before the usual time." Newman resolved to have nothing further to do with the *Merlin*.

Realizing the desperate situation that had been allowed to develop, he told the Prime Minister that he regretted not taking advice in reference to the employment of the *Victoria*. Newman also held discussions with a Captain Salt concerning his vessel *Cleopatra* on Tuesday night and Captain Salt displayed no sense of urgency. The captain said he had no doubt the *Arctic*'s boats, having the passengers on board, had out-lived the storm, as he had been for days himself in an open boat in worse weather on the coast of Ireland.

Incredibly, at this late time in the tragedy, all the Prime Minister could tell him was that, "...it was possible the Government was sending off the *Victoria*, as Mr. Shea had gone to Government House to get the Governor to dispatch her." He told Newman that he should check this out with Chandler White.

To this the American Consul replied, "If you and Mr. Shea get the *Victoria* off, to you alone would be the credit due of having done anything substantial towards the relief of the *Arctic*'s passengers and crew."

When Prime Minister Little later visited Chandler White, he learned that no offer had been made to him by Government to engage the *Victoria* in a rescue effort. Mr. White told the Prime Minister that the *Victoria* was ready for sea and he was willing to detain her for one hour to await the result of Mr. Shea's meeting with the Governor.

The Prime Minister went back to the American Consul and told him of White's offer and recommended that the Consul go immediately to Government House, "...and even if he would not undertake any responsibility in his representative character, he should express his concurrence in any arrangement which His Excellency might make with Mr. White."

Water Street in St. John's in the nineteenth century.

Just minutes after the Consul left for Government House, Mr. Shea arrived and met with Prime Minister Little to inform him that the Governor was not taking any action. He said that all the Governor offered was to consent to guarantee any agreement the Consul would make. The Prime Minister sent Mr. Shea back to Government House to again plead for action. However, when he arrived, he learned that the American Consul had not gone to Government House as promised. Under the circumstances, all that Mr. Shea could get from the Governor was a written guarantee from the Colonial Secretary for any contract the Consul would make in regards to the *Arctic*.

In a letter to the *Newfoundlander*, Prime Minister Little said:

> *Mr. White called on me near the end of the hour for an answer, and I told him that the Government would not undertake to engage the* Victoria, *and would only guarantee any undertaking which the Consul would give; and that gentleman (Chandler White) declared that he would give no undertaking, or incur no such liability, consequently he had better not permit himself to be any longer misled.*

The *Newfoundlander* was stinging in its criticism of the Government's inaction. The newspaper pointed out that authorities misled the outside world into thinking no steamers were in St. John's Harbour to respond to the disaster while, in fact, there were. The paper concluded that it was greed, inaction and bumbling that had thwarted a quick response that might have saved lives. It explained that:

> *On Tuesday evening the Government picked up a sailing vessel, which they falsely assert was the first they could procure — this being a Boston-bound craft, which we presume was instructed not to shut her eyes to any stray shipwreck she might chance to fall in with. They then dispatched Dr. Feild's (Bishop Feild) yacht, and lastly, after the appearance of our Thursday's strictures, off went the sailing clipper — all, we infer, on the principle of 'saving appearances' for in this both the Government and Mr. Newman agree!*
>
> *What we want to know is, why men who had authority to do all this, at the eleventh hour, to save appearances, were void of all power while the time yet remained for the saving of human life? And this, we opine is the question which will arise – to readers in America and England.*
>
> *It is too clear, the more this scandal is sifted and probed the more characteristic does it appear of the Government we endure. They have worked hard to vamp up their unfortunate case, but the utmost art they could bring to it has but made the truth glare with broader light. If it could have been screened by mere scheming, and the other ordinary avocations of this respected Body, doubtless they would have hit the mark. But these expedients have been uselessly employed against the fact that nothing was done at their hands to save the lives of 350 human beings. To put this out of view will require a new essay and a new cast of tactique.*

There was outrage among the people of St. John's over the handling of the response to the unfolding disaster at Newfoundland's doorsteps. Much of the criticism was directed at Governor Ker Baillie Hamilton, with public demands for his resignation.

Meanwhile, after enduring criticism for demanding an exorbitant fee to participate in the rescue operation, Chandler White sent written instructions to the Captain of the *Victoria* on the evening of October 3, ordering him to begin the search as soon as possible. In a letter to Peter Cooper, President of the Telegraph Company, Mr. White blamed Governor Ker Baillie Hamilton for the long delay in starting the rescue. He claimed the Governor would not guarantee payment for the rescue service and that he, Chandler White, finally took the matter into his own hands and sent the *Victoria* to carry out a search. One letter writer to the *Public Ledger* newspaper suggested that White's efforts were little more than a sham to cover his failure to react to the disaster instantly.

A letter critical of Governor Hamilton appeared in the *Newfoundlander* on October 7, 1854. The letter, signed 'Colonist', attributed the source of Newfoundland's public embarrassment over the incident directly on the shoulders of Ker Baillie Hamilton. It stated:

> *Your profession of philanthropy had induced a general belief that the cause of humanity at least would have elicited from you and your government some spark of energy, some vigorous effort to save the lives of hundreds of human beings known to have taken to the boats of the Arctic but a short time previous to the information reaching St. John's within fifty miles of the land, and in soundings of the waters of Your Excellency's jurisdiction.*

The writer pointed out that Governor Hamilton could have acted instantly on the basis that the *Arctic* was the National Mail Steamer in the employment of the United States of America. He added that the Governor as Commander-in-Chief and Vice Admiral had direct control over the movements of the steamship *Cleopatra*, employed in Government Service. 'Colonist' continued:

> *You permitted that vessel to remain in harbour over fifty hours, when she was quite able to be at sea, and most probably would have saved the unfortunate* Arctic *and hundreds of her ill-fated passengers and people. No effort was made by your government to expedite the steamer* Victoria, *nor has the R.M.S.* Merlin, *over which you have an absolute control by the express terms of the contract, been dispatched to the locality of the dreadful catastrophe. Some generous philanthropists have indeed sent unsuitable sailing craft; in doing so much they have done their best; but the Governor and Council of Newfoundland have emphatically declared themselves incapable. What will the British Government and the British people, who have cheerfully annually volunteered their searches for Sir John Franklin and his ill-fated crew, say to the Executive of Newfoundland? What will the generous America and her citizen people, who nobly contributed hand-in-hand to the fruitless search of the* Arctic *Expedition, say to your heartless treatment of her drowning sons and their ruined property in her National Mail Ship, within five hours sail of your residence.*

Many *Arctic* survivors, including the two originally left behind at Cappahayden, fumed after being charged four to six pounds by the Newfoundland vessel *Merlin* for their passage to Halifax, where a steamship of the Cunard Lines generously provided free transportation to their original port of destination, New York.

The full debate over Newfoundland's mishandling of the *Arctic* shipwreck did not reach the United States, and the public there were told that Newfoundland could not respond because there were no steamships in port at the time.

Not all Newfoundlanders were slow in responding to the crisis. Unable to get the support of local merchants, Bishop Feild, without charge to the Americans, gathered a crew for his yacht, the *Hawk,* and on Tuesday, October 3, sent the vessel out to search for survivors. The American Consul had hired the salt fish carrier, the ninety-three ton brig *Ann Eliza* that departed for the shipwreck scene on Monday, October 2 at 9:00 p.m. Unlike those who sought to gain financially from any rescue effort, Warren Brothers of St. John's, owners of the *Ann Eliza* unsuccessfully searched the area for survivors and, when offered payment by the American Consul, refused to accept it.

While the *Public Ledger,* a St. John's newspaper known to favour the Government in power at the time claimed that no expense had been spared and that the Government and Mr. Newman were worthy of praise, the *Newfoundlander* minced no words in putting forward its opinion. Referring to the American Consul and the Government, the *Newfoundlander* editorialized, "We are to deal with the fact that between them, they have perpetrated an atrocity which is sufficient to infamous the name of the country."

Throughout the first couple of weeks after the shipwreck of the *Arctic,* the fate of Captain Luce remained unknown. Many thought he had gone down with his ship. However, he had been rescued and taken to Quebec where he penned a letter to his employer detailing the story of the disaster. The letter dated October 14, 1854, appeared in newspapers on both sides of the Atlantic. For the first time the outside world received a detailed account of the *Arctic* Disaster. It read:

Mr. E. K. Collins, New York
Dear Sir,

It becomes my painful duty to inform you of the total loss of the noble steamship Arctic *under my command, together with your wife, son and daughter. The* Arctic *sailed from Liverpool on Wednesday, September 20, at 11 a.m. with 233 passengers and about 150 crew. Nothing special occurred during the passage until Wednesday, September 27 when at noon, on the Banks of*

Newfoundland, Latitude 46º 45' N Longitude 52º W steering W by compass, the weather being foggy during the day but generally objects being perceptible at intervals of 2 or 3/4 mile.

At noon I left the deck for the purpose of working out the position of the ship. In about fifteen minutes afterwards a cry of "Hard to Starboard" came from the officers on the deck. I rushed on deck and just got out when I felt a crash forward, and at the same moment saw a strange steamer under the starboard bow. In another moment she struck against the guards of the Arctic *and passed astern of us. The bows of the strange ship appeared to be cut off literally for about ten feet and seeing that in all probability she must sink in a few minutes, after taking a hasty glance at our own ship and believing that we were comparatively uninjured, my first impulse was to try to save the lives of those on board the stranger.*

The boats were ordered for launching and the First Officer and six men left in one of them. It was then found that our own ship was leaking fearfully. The engineers were now set to work being instructed to put on the steam pumps and the four deck pumps were worked by the passengers and crew. The ship was immediately headed for the land, which I judged to be fifty miles distant. I was compelled to leave the boat with the First Officer and his crew to take care of themselves. Several ineffectual attempts were made to stop the leaks by getting sails over the bows, but finding that the leak gained upon us very fast notwithstanding all our most powerful efforts to keep her free, I resolved to get the boats ready and have as many ladies and children placed in them as they could carry. But no sooner had the attempt been made than the firemen and others rushed into them in spite of all opposition.

Seeing this state of things, I ordered the boat astern to be kept in readiness until order could be restored. To my dismay, I saw the rope in the bow had been cut and they soon disappeared in the fog. Another boat was broken down by persons rushing at the davits by which many were precipitated into the sea. This occurred while I had been engaged in getting the starboard guard boat ready to launch, of which I had placed the second officer in charge. When the same fearful scene was enacted as with the first boat, men leaping from the top of the rail, a height of twenty feet, bruising and maiming those who were in the boat hanging alongside. I then gave orders to the Second Officer, Mr. Baalham, to let go and drop astern of us, keeping under or near the stern to be ready to take on board women and children as soon as the fires were out and the engines stopped.

My attention was then drawn to the other quarter boat, which I found broken down but still hanging by one tackle. A rush was also made for her, when some fifteen passengers jumped in and cut the tackle and were soon out of sight. I now found not a seaman or carpenter was left on board. The only officer left was Mr. Dorian, Third Officer, who aided me and with the assistance of many passengers who deserve the greatest praise for their coolness and energy did all in their power up to the last moment when the ship sank.

The chief engineer, with several of his assistants had taken the smallest of our deck boats and had with fifteen persons pulled away before the ship sank. We had succeeded in getting the fore and main yards and two top gallant yards overboard, together with such other small spars and materials as we could collect, when I became fully convinced that the ship must go down in a very few minutes and that not a moment was to be lost in getting the spars lashed together to form the raft, to do which it became necessary to get out the lifeboat, the only boat left. This being accomplished, I placed Mr. Dorian in charge of the boat taking care to keep back the oars, so that the boat might not be taken away as I still hoped to get most of the women and children in this boat at least.

We had made considerable progress in the connecting of the spars when an alarm was given that the ship was sinking and the boat was shoved off without oars or any means of helping themselves and when the ship sank the boat was probably 1/8 mile away. Instantly, at about 15 minutes to 5 p.m. the ship went down carrying every soul on board with her. I soon found myself on the surface again and after a brief struggling with my helpless child in my arms I again felt myself impelled downward to a great depth and before I reached the surface again I had nearly perished and had lost my hold on my child. As I again struggled to the surface of the water, a most awful and heart-rending scene presented itself to my view, women and children struggling together amidst pieces of wreckage of every kind, calling on each other and God to assist them. Such another appalling scene may God preserve me from ever witnessing. I was in the act of trying to save my child again when a portion of the paddle box came crashing up edgewise and just grazed my head and fell with its whole weight on the head of my darling child. In another moment, I beheld him, a lifeless corpse on the surface of the waves.

I succeeded with eleven others in getting on top of a piece of the paddle box. One who found that all could not be supported by this piece of the paddle box let go and swam to another piece nearby. The others remained in the water until one by one they were relieved by death. We stood up to our knees in water at forty-five degrees and frequently the sea broke directly over us.

We were soon separated from our friends on other parts of the wreck and passed a terrible night, each one expecting every hour to be his last.

At last, the long wished for morning came accompanied by fog. Not a living soul but our own party to be seen of which only seven men were left. In the course of the morning we saw water casks and other things belonging to our ill-fated ship, but could get nothing that would afford us any relief and our raft was rapidly sinking as it absorbed water. About noon, Mr. S.M. Woodruff breathed his last and all the others except Mr. George F. Allen of N.Y. and myself began to suffer excruciatingly for want of water. In this respect we were very much favoured although we had not a drop of fresh water on the raft. The day continued foggy except just at noon, as near as we could judge, when we had a clear horizon for about half an hour.

Nothing could be seen but water and sky. Night came on thick and dreary and our minds were fully made up that neither of us would again see the day. Very soon three more of our suffering party were washed off and sank to rise no more, leaving only Mr. Allen and myself. Feeling myself very much exhausted, I sat down for the first time about eight o'clock on a trunk which had providentially been found among the wreckage. In this way I slept a little through the night and became somewhat refreshed. About an hour before daylight, we saw a vessel's light near us and all three of us exerted ourselves to the utmost of our strength in hailing her until we became quite exhausted. In about a quarter of an hour, the light disappeared in the eastward. Soon after daylight, a barque hove in sight to the northwest, the fog having lightened a little. She was apparently steering for us, but in a short time, she seemed to have changed her course and we were again doomed to disappointment, yet I felt a hope that some of our fellow sufferers might have been seen and rescued by them.

Shortly after we had given up all hope of being discovered or rescued by the barque, a ship was discovered to the eastward steering directly for us. We now watched her with intense anxiety as she approached. The wind changing caused her to alter course several points. About noon they fortunately discovered a man on a raft near them and succeeded in saving him, the second mate jumping overboard and making a rope fast to the man on the raft and he was

*drawn aboard. He proved to be a Frenchman who had
been a passenger on board the steamer with which we had
collided. He informed the Captain that others were near
on pieces of wreckage and on going aloft, he saw us and
three others. We were the first to which the boat was sent
and were safely aboard at 3 p.m. The next picked up was
James Smith, a second-class passenger on the* Arctic. *The
others saved were five of our firemen. The ship proved to
be the* Cambria *of Quebec, from Glasgow for Montreal,
commanded by Captain John Russell who had commanded
the British barque* Jessie Stevens, *and was rescued from the
wreck of that vessel by Captain Nye of the Collins
steamship* Pacific, *as will be remembered.*

*Of Captain Russell it would be scarcely possible to say
enough in his praise for the kind treatment we received
from him during the time we were on board his ship. His
own comforts he gave up in every respect for our relief.
The Rev. Mr. Walker and wife and another gentleman, who
were passengers on the* Cambria, *have been unending in
their efforts to promote our comfort. To them and all on
board we shall ever owe a debt of gratitude for their
unbounded kindness to us. From the Frenchman who was
picked up, we learned that the steamer with which we had
been in contact was the screw steamer* Vesta, *from St.
Pierre and McQuelon, heading for Granville, France.*

As near as we could learn, the Vesta *was steering
E.S.E. and was crossing our course within two points with
all sail set, the land being W by N. Her anchor stock, about
7 by 4 inches, was drawn through the bows of the* Arctic
*about 18 inches above the water line. An immense hole
had been made at the same instant by the fluke of the
anchor, about 2 feet below the water line, raking fore and
aft the planks and finally breaking the chains and leaving
the stock remaining in and through the side of the* Arctic. *It
is more than likely that so much of the French steamer's
bows had been crushed in that some of the heavy longitu-*

dinal pieces of iron running through the ship may have been drawn through our sides causing the loss of the Arctic *and I fear many valuable lives.*

I have safely arrived at Quebec but am without a penny in the world wherewith to help myself. With sincere gratitude to those from whom I have received such unbounded kindness since I have been providentially thrown among them, I am about to separate from them and go to New York — a home of sorrow. I learned from the doctor at quarantine, last evening, that the Vesta *had reached St. John's with several passengers from the* Arctic *but could not learn the particulars. As soon as I can get on shore I shall make arrangements to leave for New York with the least possible delay. I shall take the steamer for Montreal this afternoon.*

"I am respectfully
– James C. Luce."

It took seventy-two hours after the *Arctic* went down for word of the disaster to reach St. John's. In that time the lifeboats rowing away from the scene, not knowing which direction to go, could have covered a lot of miles. The situation required a swift rescue effort with steamships that could travel at a fast speed and cover large areas in a short time. Unfortunately, such a rescue was not mounted because those with power to do so failed to act. Of the 383 passengers and crew on the *Arctic* only eighty-six persons survived.[6] There was not a woman or a child among the survivors.[7] This sad fact was attributed to the failure of many crewmen to put women and children first in evacuating the ship and seizing lifeboats for themselves.

The *Vesta* was forced to remain in St. John's until the spring while Newfoundland's genius shipbuilder, Michael Kearney,

6. Other accounts of the disaster have reported varying figures regarding the number of persons lost in the tragedy. H.M. Mosdell, in *When was That?* reported 350 lives lost. *Rivalry in the Atlantic* reported 322 lives lost and *Women and Children Last*, the most authoritative account of the Arctic Disaster reported 297 lost.
7. The total number of people reported to be on the *Arctic* has also varied. *Rivalry on the Atlantic* reported 408 while Women and Children Last reported 383.

repaired the damages to the vessel. The French Naval vessel *Camelion* took the *Vesta*'s survivors home to France, leaving the captain and a skeleton crew to look after its interests and return the vessel to France when repairs were completed. The captain found it necessary to publish advertisements in St. John's newspapers advising the public he would not be responsible for bills incurred by his crew.

For his leadership and courage throughout the ordeal, the French Government made Captain Duchesne a *Chevalier of the Legion of Honour*.

In the aftermath of the disaster, American newspapers speculated on what action could have been taken by Captain Luce to avoid the tragedy or lessen the numbers of those lost in the tragedy. One such suggestion came from a Captain Ericsson who felt the ship should have stopped as soon as it had become apparent she could not reach the Newfoundland coast and the water blown out of the boilers so that their great capacity might have been utilized as flotation tanks to keep the wreck from sinking. Another person suggested that the ship should have been backed towards the Newfoundland coast to reduce the flow of water through the damaged area near the bow.[8]

The most positive result of the *Arctic* Disaster was the new shipping laws that established sea-lanes across the Atlantic.

In the months following the tragedy, there were several newspaper reports of people who refused to board the *Arctic* because they had premonitions of the disaster. One could only wonder about the reaction of the gypsy fortune teller who foretold Brown's death, when she later picked up a newspaper reporting on the loss of the *Arctic* and 297 people, among whom was one of the owners of the Collins Liner Company, the William Brown whose palm she had read just months before.

8. Commander W. Mack Angas, USN, author *Rivalry On The Atlantic*, 1939.

Chapter 3

Terror in
Newfoundland Waters

Fishermen Face Sea Monster

On September 18, 1966, the United States Naval Oceanographic Research vessel *San Pablo* was operating in waters 120 miles east northeast of Cape Bonavista, Newfoundland, when the crew noticed something unusual breaching the water within viewing distance of the vessel.

The spectacle that followed was something no man on the boat had ever witnessed, and not likely would again. A life and death battle was being played out between a sperm whale and a giant squid. Which sea creature won the battle is not known, but this was not the first battle of this nature to be witnessed by man.

In 1875, F.T. Bullen, British journalist, was a passenger on the whaling ship *Cachelot*, and watched through his binoculars an encounter between a giant squid and a sperm whale. That incident inspired Newfoundland poet E. J. (Ned) Pratt to write his epic poem *The Cachelot* in 1926, in which he immortalized the battle between two monsters of the sea.

The giant squid, known by other names including Kracken, Devil Fish and Cuttlefish, has terrorized Newfoundland fishermen over the centuries, and has been the inspiration in many tales and myths. According to the late Dr. Fred Aldrich of Memorial University, St. John's, Newfoundland, a world authority on the giant squid, the first clear historical reference to the creature was made in 1555 by Olaus Magnus, Archbishop of Upsala, Sweden, who described a monstrous fish seen off the coast of Norway. The Archbishop noted, "Their forms are horrible, their heads are square, and they have sharp and long horns round about, like a tree rooted up by the roots."

It was Olaus Magnus, according to Dr. Aldrich, who coined the word 'Kracken' in describing the giant squid. For more than 300 years after Magnus wrote about the Kracken, there was practically no scientific work to verify the existence of this sea creature. Sailors around the world told exaggerated, and often mythical tales of the monster squid. Jules Verne in *Twenty Thousand Leagues Under the Sea* described an encounter between Captain Nemo and the crew of the Nautilus with a giant Kracken.

The author Osmond P. Breland observed:

Since Homer's Odyssey, *with its account of Ulysses'
battle with Scylla, who was evidently a giant squid, stories
of bloodthirsty, many-armed monsters have been told by
seafaring men.*[1]

By the end of the nineteenth century, Newfoundland became
the world's focal point for knowledge and evidence that proved the
mythical Devil Fish, or Kracken, really existed.

In 1873, when two fishermen and a boy were fishing in
Conception Bay a few miles north of St. John's, the existence of the
sea-monster called the Devil Fish was only a tall tale. By the end
of the day they had the solid proof the world scientific community
was looking for to prove the existence of the creature. It also
marked a day of terror that remained instilled in their memories for
a lifetime.

It was October 26, when Theophilus Piccott, his twelve-year-
old son Tom, and Daniel Squires, Theo's fishing partner, set out for
the fishing grounds in the Tickle near Bell Island. Tom was proud
to be at the tiller, and enjoying working with his father, when suddenly terror struck. Dan Squires had noticed a dark brownish
object floating a short distance from the boat. After he pointed out
the item to Theo, young Tom was told to steer the boat towards the
object. Both men agreed that it was likely some kind of wreckage.
When the boat drew near enough, Dan prodded the object with his
boat hook.

*I gently lowered the grapnel down
Towards its mighty jaws,
And all at once some lengthy arms
Was wrapped around the claws.
I pulled away with all my might–
To discover was my wish*

1. Breland, Osmon P., "Devils of the Deep {re: 1873 discovery of giant squid}" *Science
Digest*, October 1952. 32 pp 31-33.

Carter-Fitzgerald Photography
Author Jack Fitzgerald, discussing the *giant squid*, in the television series *Legends and Lore of the North Atlantic*, produced by Pope Productions, St. John's, NL and hosted by Gordon Pinsent. This series is shown on the Mystery, Global and Prime television channels.

What had devoured my grapnel
Such a monster looking fish!
(My Adventure With a Giant Squid, T. E. Tuck)[2]

Suddenly, the dormant floating object turned into a raging sea monster that sent waves of terror down the spines of the three fishermen. They had come face to face with the mythical Devil Fish. The creature swiftly emerged from the water, and launched an attack upon the little fishing boat. What appeared to be a dozen snake-like tentacles, ranging between ten and thirty-five feet in length, lashed towards the boat with two of the tentacles gripping around it. The body of the creature measured ten feet long and eight feet wide. The two men were almost mesmerized by the two large black eyes, about eight inches each in diameter, which fixed on them. A bulk of tissue in the center of the head opened, and a large horny parrot-like beak projected, opening and closing and viciously attacking the gunwale of the boat.

2. *Newfoundland Quarterly*, March 1954, Vol. 53 (1) pp 18

One of the tentacles fastened to the boat while the other encircled it and began to drag it down into the ocean. Water began pouring into the boat, but the two men, still in a state of terror, did not move to fight off the attack.

It was at this moment, when death seemed imminent, that young Tom regained his composure and launched a direct attack on the Devil Fish. He grabbed a tomahawk lying on the bottom of the boat and began chopping at the thirty-five-foot long tentacle holding the vessel. After severing the tentacle that encircled the little craft, Tom succeeded in chopping off the second tentacle that had attached itself to the boat. Tom single-handedly defeated the creature, which retreated down into the ocean while emitting a darkened fluid to hide its trail as it disappeared from view.

Tom had the presence of mind to make sure that the two severed tentacles were in the boat before his father and Dan Squires rowed to shore in fear that at any time the creature might attack again. When the trio arrived home in Portugal Cove, Tom left the shorter tentacle near the front door to his home where it was dragged away and eaten by dogs. He took the long arm and preserved it as a trophy of his victory over the creature. His action on that date contributed to the scientific world community being able to move the existence of a giant squid from myth to reality.

The story of the terror on the Tickle near Bell Island spread throughout Portugal Cove, and attracted the interest of the Anglican Minister in the community. He visited the Piccott family, and after hearing the first-hand account of the adventure, and seeing the tentacle cut from the creature by young Tom, the minister suggested Tom take it to Dr. Moses Harvey in St. John's. Dr. Harvey was Minister at St. Andrew's Presbyterian Church, and known internationally for his interest in science and nature.

Rev. Dr. Harvey's interest in giant squid was sparked by stories he had heard from Newfoundland fishermen about a creature they called 'the big squid' which had horns, or arms that measured from twenty to thirty feet in length. The story that truly captured his attention was a fisherman's tale of a narrow escape he and two others had on the coast of Labrador.

The little vessel of some twenty-five or thirty tons in which they were in, in the still water of a harbour, suddenly began to sink, until the deck was nearly on a level with the water. There was no water in her hold to account for this. In alarm, they launched their boat to escape. This startled a big squid that had attached itself by its suckers to the bottom of the vessel, and was dragging it under the waves. The moment it relaxed its hold, the vessel rose to its former position, and the men saw the squid, some thirty or forty feet in length, shooting rapidly through the water, and in a few minutes, was out of sight.³

After hearing this story, Harvey became determined that he would someday capture, or find a giant squid. He had dreams of being able to solve the mystery of centuries.

Since Tom was eager to profit from the rare item in his possession, the next day he and his dad placed the tentacle in a tub on their wagon, which they ordinarily used to bring supplies to and from the city, and set out to bring the piece of scientific evidence to the Plymouth Road residence of Dr. Harvey. When they arrived and showed Dr. Harvey the monster's tentacle, he immediately recognized that this could be the evidence the scientific world was seeking to prove the existence of a giant squid. Harvey recalled:

How my heart pounded as I drew out of the tub in which he carried it, coil after coil, to the length of nineteen feet, the dusky red member, strong and tough as leather, about as thick as a man's wrist. I knew at a glance it was one of the tentacles or long arms of the ancient's Kraken, or modern giant cuttle fish. Eureka!⁴

Young Tom was happy to receive $10.00 from Dr. Harvey for the specimen, and Theo Piccott agreed to have Dr. Harvey visit him at Portugal Cove next day to discuss the encounter with the creature.

3. Rev. Moses Harvey, "A Sea Monster Unmasked, 1899," *Science Digest.*
4. Rev. Moses Harvey, "A Sea Monster Unmasked, 1899," *Science Digest.*.

When Dr. Harvey arrived at Portugal Cove, Theo, Dan Squires and young Tom were present to answer his questions. When Tom finished telling his remarkable story, he casually added, "I thought I was done for by the big squid." In his notes Dr. Harvey recorded that Tom had regarded the episode as a lark, but the two men had not recovered from the terrorizing encounter. He said that the senior Piccott and Dan Squires showed fear in their eyes as they described the creature. Dan Squires said, "It had eyes as big as saucers, gleaming with fury, and a fierce parrot-like beak that was ready to tear us apart."[5]

They estimated that the length of the creature was sixty feet, and its head was as round as a six-gallon keg. Stories had long been told among Newfoundland fishermen of monster-size squids, but Dr. Harvey had never encountered, or heard of one being sighted in Conception Bay. After examining the tentacle, and considering the information given to him by the three witnesses, he concluded the giant squid weighed about 1,000 pounds with tentacles as long as thirty-five feet. He arranged to have the tentacle photographed, and then began writing his scientific paper.

Dr. Harvey later described his thoughts at the time:

> *I was now the possessor of one of the rarest curiosities in the whole animal kingdom — the veritable arm of the hitherto mythical devilfish about whose existence, naturalists had been disputing for centuries. I knew that I held in my hand the key of the great mystery, and that a new chapter would be added to natural history. I was thus, by good fortune, the discoverer of a new and remarkable species of fish, the very existence of which had been widely and scornfully denied, and had never been absolutely proved.*

Although Harvey was thrilled over having the tentacle of a giant squid, he lamented not been able to obtain a complete creature. He wrote in his notes:

5. Harrington, Michael F. , "The Sea Monsters in Conception Bay (re: giant squid, 1873-1877)" *Atlantic Guardian*, June 1957, Vol. 14 (6), pp 23-29.

Destiny, however, had something better in store for me than the acquisition of the tentacle. Only three weeks after the event described, a message reached me, which threw me into a perfect fever of excitement. Another devilfish had been brought ashore in perfect condition at a place called Logy Bay, a few miles north of St. John's.[6]

Dr. Harvey wasted little time in getting to Logy Bay. The fishermen were excited about their find and were eager to talk about their experience. Harvey was delighted to see that, with the exception of the head, the remainder of the creature was intact. He knew that he had something that no museum in the world possessed.

The Logy Bay fishermen captured the creature after it became entangled in their net. When they began hauling in the net, they realized they had something more than fish in it. The net was much heavier than usual, and when they moved it, whatever was trapped in it began a ferocious battle to escape. The net was shaken, moved and pulled in all directions.

When the fishermen got the net to the surface, they were astonished to see a sea-monster struggling to free itself. The huge eyes and wriggling snake-like tentacles struck fear in the Logy Bay fishermen. Several tentacles extended through openings in the net, and sought to grasp the boat. They were about to release the net when one man regained his composure, drew his splitting knife, and slashed the blade across the creature and severed most of its head. With the creature now dead, they managed to get it to shore. The man who had killed the monster told Harvey he would not wish to repeat the experience of the half-hour battle with the giant squid for all the money in the world.

Harvey offered the men 'a few dollars' for the creature, and after getting it on board his wagon, took it to his home in St. John's, where after storing it in brine, he placed it in a shed in his back garden. Word about the capture of a devilfish spread rapidly and crowds began visiting Dr. Harvey's shed to get a glimpse of the historic find.

6. Rev. Moses Harvey, "A Sea Monster Unmasked," *Science Digest* 1899.

Author Jack Fitzgerald researching archival material.

Some called it this, some called it that,
As it lay there on shore,
But the oldest man that was on the strand,
Never saw the like before.
I've seen all kinds of funny fish,
All kinds of shapes and forms–
I'd call this one the Devil,
But he has too many horns!
(My Adventure With a Giant Squid by T. E. Tuck)

This creature was smaller than the one encountered by the Portugal Cove fishermen. Its body measured about six feet long, and the tentacles were up to twenty-four feet. The creature's total length with tentacles extended in opposite directions was fifty feet.

Dr. Harvey completed his study of the specimens and presented his papers, along with the giant squid specimens, to Professor A. E. Verril of Yale University, a world authority on Cephalopods. Based on Harvey's papers, Professor Verril wrote a series of scientific papers on 'The Cephalopods of North America', which gave Harvey international recognition. Dr. Harvey noted in his records,

"Professor Verril did me the honour of naming the specimen Architeuthis Harveyi in honour of its discoverer."

Rev. Harvey also sent copies of his papers to Sir William Dawson of McGill University who presented them to the National Historic Society of Montreal.

The noted Swedish Ichthyologist (scientist who studies fish) Jean Louis Agassiz wrote Harvey expressing his delight in the discovery, and asked permission to examine the creature. Unfortunately, Agassiz died weeks later on December 12, 1873, without getting a chance to visit Dr. Harvey.

Dr. Harvey began receiving many requests from those wanting to purchase a giant squid, including offers from P. T. Barnum owner of *The Greatest Show on Earth*.

Around the same time that Dr. Harvey was preparing his scientific paper, and getting ready to ship his specimens to Professor Verril, another giant squid turned up on the north shore of Newfoundland. Businessman Archibald Munn took possession of the parts of this creature from the fishermen who caught it. The parts saved consisted of jaws, which were four inches long, and suckers which were an inch in diameter. Mr. Munn sent these specimens to the National Museum at Washington, D.C., United States. The Munn items were also studied by Professor Verril.[7]

During the appearances of giant squid in Newfoundland waters in 1873, the mystery of the Sea Devil's Rock (Bishop's Rock) in Conception Bay, Newfoundland, was solved, but not without a terrorizing confrontation with two St. John's fishermen.

The Legend of Sea Devil's Rock in Conception Bay became reality for Sam Wilney and Pat Daly of St. John's during October 1873. Bishop's Rock, Conception Bay, was renamed Sea Devil's Rock by St. John's fishermen after two fishermen, working near the rock on separate occasions, disappeared, leaving their boats, equipment, and not a trace of what might have happened to either of them.

7. *Harper's New Monthly Magazine*, February 1874.

While most fishermen avoided the area because of a belief that something evil was connected with it, Sam Wilney and Pat Daly anchored their boat there one day at a respectable distance from the Rock. Wilney was searching for his axe to repair an oar when Daly was startled to see something in the water near the rock, surface, and then disappear.

He shouted, "Faith! If I believed in the sea-serpent, I should say there's one over there now."

"What nonsense are you talking?" Wilney said. "You're up to some game."

"No, be Jasus!" Daly declared. "I swear I saw a great long thing rise out of the water, wriggling and twisting about like a serpent. Hanged if I don't begin to think there's something uncanny about that rock."

Wilney disregarded Daly's alert, and after fixing the oar, rowed round the rock. It was a calm day on Conception Bay with not even a ripple on the water. About twenty-five feet to the side of the little fishing boat, which was halfway to the Sea Devil's Rock, Wilney noticed what appeared to be a big bunch of seaweed.

Wilney described the terror of the next moments:

I could see some dark streaks like strings of seaweed floating out through the water, and I says to Pat, "It's nothing, but a lot of seaweed." Suddenly, out like a flash shot something from beneath the water, and lay across the middle of the boat. It came so quickly, it was simply like lightning. All we saw was that something had made a great leap, and the next thing we knew was that there was a thing like a long serpent lying across the boat, making it rock from side to side, and dragging it bodily towards the rock.

Before you could look around, in a flash comes another one with a wriggle in the air, and a sort of flying leap. Then there were two long brown things like snakes lying right across the boat, and dragging it towards the rock. I could see twenty feet or more of each of them, and the boat was nearly tipped over.

The creature pulled the boat until the gunwale was near the water, and then it rushed over the side into the boat. I sat like a stuck pig, when Pat cries out, "Chop it off, man! Chop now! Chop for your life!"

Sam grabbed the axe and began chopping furiously at the creature. He succeeded in cutting off two of the tentacles that had seized the boat, and they fell wriggling to the floor. However, the attack was not yet over.

Sam Wilney described the next few moments:

I got hold of the paddles, and got the boat's head round to row away, when up out of the water rose, not one, or two, but four or five great wriggling snakes, and a big thing as large as a tub, with two eyes as big as soup plates. Then and there, I knew what it was. It was a tremendous devilfish, and it had been lying just under the water, hanging onto the rock with two or three of its arms.

Sam had seen many small squid, and on occasion had one jump out of the water and fasten onto his arm or hand. He could easily free himself from one by squeezing its windpipe, and it would let go immediately. Sam's experience with small squid convinced him that the monster squid in front of him was about to leap at him. He thought that if the creature made the sudden leap, it would capsize the boat, and he and Pat wouldn't have a chance.

"Thank heaven, he didn't!" exclaimed Sam. "He only gave a great plunge, and disappeared, leaving the water all round us as black as ink. Well, I thought he'd likely come up again, so you bet I rowed. Yes, sir! And I never stopped 'til I felt the bow touch the shore, and then I think I fainted."

Pat drew a long breath and said, "Be Jasus! But that were a near squeak! It's clear now what became of those other poor devils. Arrah, but we've got something here to prove we didn't dream it all. Anyhow. Let's take 'em ashore."[8]

---

8. Frank Aubrey, "A Newfoundland Terror," *Fore's Sporting & Sketches*, 1896, Vol. 13, pp. 10-15.

Frank Aubrey, author of *A Newfoundland Terror*, noted, at the end of the story, that he had verified the fishermen's story, and had viewed the tentacles cut from the giant squid at the Museum in St. John's, Newfoundland.

Four years later, another giant squid was driven ashore at Catalina during a severe windstorm that struck Newfoundland on September 22, 1877. The bewildered creature of the deep tried to escape by swimming backward, and stuck its tail on a rock, which rendered it powerless. An unidentified fisherman, watching it from shore, described its actions:

> *In its desperate effort to escape, the ten arms darted out in all directions, lashing the water into a foam. The thirty-foot long tentacles, in particular, made lively play as it shot them out, and endeavored to grasp onto something with their powerful suckers so that it could drag itself into deep water. When it was exhausted and with the tide receding, a group of fishermen, who had gathered on shore, approached it.*

The fishermen kept a respectable distance from the creature as they tried to determine if it was dead or alive. Once satisfied it was dead, and not able to harm them, two fishermen from the group took possession of it. On September 26, they took it by boat to St. John's. News of the presence of the dead monster fish in St. John's drew widespread interest, and crowds began showing up at the harbour wharf to see it. In response to the public show of curiosity, the government allowed the fishermen to display it in a drill shed near the harbour. [9]

The people came from far and near,
To see the giant squid,
Saying, you can make your fortune
If you only use your head,

---

9. Don Morris, *Evening Telegram*, St. John's, Newfoundland, September 13, 1963.

So I then put up a poster
So as everyone would know
If they want to see a devilfish
It would cost ten cents a show.
I collected fifteen dollars
From those who came around,
And later sold the whole darn works
To a businessman in town.
He paid me fifteen dollars more;
Thirty dollars was the sum
I didn't make my fortune,
But I had a barrel of fun.
(My Adventure with a Giant Squid, *by T.E. Tuck*)

When removed from the water the creature's color was a dusky red, but soon after it turned white. It was similar in dimensions and features to the two, which were studied by Dr. Moses Harvey in 1873. Many groups expressed an interest in purchasing this giant squid, and it was sold to the New York Aquarium for $500. The Aquarium housed the creature in a specially-built glass tank that measured twenty-five feet long, five feet wide and three and a half feet deep.

On October 27, 1877, the *Canadian Illustrated News* reported:

The latest addition to the remarkable collection of the New York Aquarium is by far the most curious of specimens. It is a monster cuttle-fish (squid) made familiar to the public by Victor Hugo as the devilfish. It is a most horrible looking creature.

In 1882, a giant squid taken from Newfoundland waters was on display at Worth's Museum in the Bowery, New York, which was one of the most popular museums in America in the nineteenth century.

The Museum distributed posters around New York to promote the attraction, which it described as a 'Devil Fish' from Newfoundland. According to the St. John's *Evening Mercury*,

January 5, 1882, "A huge Woodcut on the head of the advertising placard showed ten arms flung out, two of them grasping and curling round two human beings who are writhing in agony." Newspaper competition in St. John's was strong in those days, and often the animosity between competing editors spilled over into the daily news items. In this instance, the editor at the *Evening Mercury* took a swipe at the editor of the *Evening Telegram*. He stated:

Some people here, who have examined this woodcut, say that one of the sufferers grappled by the Devil Fish has a striking resemblance to the head editor of the Evening Telegram, *his photograph having been forwarded along with the fish, but we are unable to concur in this opinion. The figure in the woodcut is not nearly as handsome.*

The people said they could not think,
Or at least, believe their eyes;
That a little squid could grow so big —
To such tremendous size.
But after we had that earthquake,
The squids got on the bum,
And I believe to God, with all my heart,
They were all knocked into one.
(My Adventure with a Giant Squid, *by T. E. Tuck)*

Giant squid were more plentiful in Newfoundland waters than many thought. Osmond P. Breland, Science Journalist, noted in his writings, "A flash of twenty-five to thirty of the giants were found at one time. All of them were cut up for bait by members of a fishing fleet." Breland did not elaborate on this incident in his article.

In 1912, two brothers, Josiah and Henry Sheppard, set out from Lark Harbor to go fishing. The older brother, Henry, used his motorboat to tow Josiah's dory to the fishing grounds. Upon arriving there, Josiah transferred to the dory, and Henry slackened the towline which allowed the dory to drift 200 yards.

While attaching bait to his line, Josiah became temporarily paralyzed with fear when a large creature suddenly confronted him, the likes of which he had never seen before. The creature's head came high out of the water, and its huge eyes fixated on the bait-codfish in the bottom of the boat. This action was followed by the creature's tentacles leaping from the water, and the longest one wrapping around the dory. The head then submerged and began dragging the dory beneath the water. The quick action knocked Josiah off balance, and he fell into the water. Josiah shouted to his brother for help. While he struggled to keep afloat, the dory resurfaced bottom up. The boy regained control of his thoughts, and knew he had to get out of the water while waiting for his brother to arrive. He managed to climb up on the dory, and not long after, Henry arrived, and helped him get into the motorboat.

The Sheppards, fearing a return of the giant creature, abandoned their fishing efforts and returned to shore. Henry and Josiah knew they had encountered a giant squid. Josiah was convinced that had it not been for the bait in his boat, the giant squid would have attacked him.[10]

In 1937, Constable W. Davis, a Newfoundland Ranger, recorded that two fishermen from Tack's Beach had to run their boat ashore to save it from sinking after it had been attacked by a huge fish with teeth like arrowheads. Davis noted:

> *On Saturday last, whilst Joseph Warren and his hired man were hauling their cod net, a huge brown-backed fish seized the keel forward and almost overturned the boat. Letting go the stern, the fish seized the keel amidships, and then near the stern, lifting the boat so much out of the water that the bow went under, and a lot of water was shipped.[11]*

The men decided to head for land, and to beach the boat, which was rapidly sinking. The move succeeded in breaking the boat

10. "Attacked by a Sea Monster" (re: 1912 devil fish/giant squid encounter, Lark Harbour) *Downhomer*, October 1999, Vol. 12 (5), p.85.
11. *Evening Telegram*, October 1937.

away from the creature. When the bottom of the boat was examined, it showed that the keel had been almost torn from the timbers. Three of the monster's broken teeth were found embedded in the keel. These were sent to Dr. McPherson of the Newfoundland Fisheries Research Office, but could not be identified.

During the 1940s there were sightings of the giant squids in the Placentia Bay area. Abe Brinston, a fisherman from Arch Cove, was confronted by one of the creatures. He was trying to repair his boat's motor, which had broken down while he was fishing, when a monster suddenly surfaced very close to his boat. He described it as, "...nothing less than the devil himself. It tried to climb into my boat, and was holding the boat with a monstrous set of claws."

Brinston battled and defeated the monster with his boat hook, which he used to cut the claws and head off the creature. On his trip to shore he thought, "Nobody will ever believe this story."

The next day, Clayton Stacey, a fisherman from Sound Island near Arch Cove, encountered a similar creature. The description given by Stacey was similar to that given in the community by Brinston. Stacey was carrying a gun, which he used to fight off the monster. He said he hit the creature with a shot, and it disappeared beneath the water, followed by a trail of blood. Stacey did not feel he had killed the creature.

When word spread throughout Placentia Bay that there was a wounded monster in the area, fishermen began carrying weapons. Several days passed and another monster from the sea, perhaps the wounded one shot by Stacey, showed up near the beach at New Harbour. One man who witnessed it told an *Evening Telegram* reporter, "It was big around as a puncheon, and an awful length. It tried to pull itself up on the rocks close to shore. Each time, it slipped back into the water."[12]

A Mr. Glavine, while jigging for cod off Philip Head, Notre Dame Bay, NL, snagged a giant squid in 1957. It was about a meter below his boat. Mr. Glavine cut the line before the creature could react, and it quickly disappeared.

12. *Untold Stories of Newfoundland*, Jack Fitzgerald, Creative Publishers, 2004.

While swimming near the surface, a giant squid is often mistaken for a monster sea serpent, and is often described by those seeing it as a very long snake-like creature. The *New York Sun* on November 30, 1879, explained why someone seeing a giant squid swimming might think they are watching a monster serpent. The article said:

> *The giant squid while swimming with portions of its body visible above the water is sometimes mistaken for a monster serpent. While swimming, the giant squid brings its many arms together in a line, thus affording the least possible resistence, and propels itself by ejecting water from its syphon. Giant squids move with an up and down motion exposing parts of their bodies like a snake going through water.*[13]

Not all encounters in Newfoundland waters with the giant squid were without casualties. In 1874, Bill Darling was the only Newfoundlander serving on the *Peril*, a 150-ton schooner. While sailing in Newfoundland waters, the crew sighted an unknown creature floating near the surface of the water a short distance from the boat.

The *Peril*'s captain, James Flood, described his action after seeing the creature, "I went into my cabin for my rifle, and as I was preparing to fire, Bill Darling came on deck, and looking at the monster said, 'Have a care master, that ere's a squid and will capsize us if we hurt him.' Smiling at the idea, I let fly and hit the squid, and with that, he shook. There was a great ripple all around him, and he began to move."

"Out with your axes and knives," shouted Bill, "and cut away any of him that comes aboard. Look alive and Lord, help us."

Captain Flood replied, "I had never seen a giant squid before and was not aware of the danger. I did not give any orders, and it was no use touching the helm or ropes to get out of the way. By

13. "Sea Serpent Accounted for in 1879 {re: Sighting of giant squid and Octopus; covers 1861-1879} *Shortis,* 1879," Vol. 3 (469), p 411.

then, Bill and three other men had axes, and were looking over the side at the advancing monster. We could see a large oblong mass, moving by jerks, just under the surface of the water, and an enormous train followed." The monster was about half the size of the vessel, according to Edward R. Snow, author of *Mysteries and Adventures Along the Atlantic Coast.* He estimated it to be about 100 feet long.

Captain Flood remarked, "Quickly, the brute struck, and the ship quivered under its thud. In another moment, monstrous arms, like trees, seized the vessel, and she keeled over. In yet another moment, the monster was aboard and squeezed in between the masts."

"Slash for your life," Bill Darling shouted.

The slashing seemed to have little effect on the creature as it slipped its large body overboard, and pulled the vessel down with him.

Bill Darling said, "We were thrown into the water, and just as I went over, I caught sight of one of the crew, squashed up between the masts and one of those awful arms. For a few seconds, our ship lay on her beam ends, then filled, and went down."

The schooner *Stratbowen* was near enough to witness the giant squid attack. It moved into the area in time to rescue Flood and the surviving members of his crew.

In 1963, Doctor Fred Aldrich initiated an effort to capture a giant squid for scientific study. Based on his research, Dr. Aldrich put forward a theory that the giant squid surfaced in Newfoundland waters in thirty-year cycles. He concentrated his efforts during autumn, and launched a publicity campaign inviting people to report any sightings of the giant squid. The appeal was successful, and he received many reports of sightings of the creature, and in a few cases, reports that a giant squid had been stranded on shore. Reports of sightings came from Portugal Cove, Harbour Main, King's Cove, Dildo, Coomb's Cove, Fortune Bay, Chapel Arm, Deer Island and Lance Cove.

During 1964 and 1965, Dr. Aldrich acquired five giant squid. The first and largest was taken during October 1964, at Conche, White Bay on Newfoundland's Northern Peninsula. It weighed 330 pounds, was thirty feet long with tentacles twenty-one feet in length. A fisherman who was hauling wood at Cape Fox discovered this creature, and he towed it to Conche. The man had not heard of Dr. Aldrich's appeal. The employees at the Bait Depot in Conche were aware of Dr. Aldrich's interest, and they contacted him regarding the find. He arranged for Eastern Provincial Airways to fly the creature to St. John's.

Several weeks later, other giant squid similar in size to the one taken at Conche, were found at Chapel Arm, and at Lance Cove, Trinity Bay. In November 1964, one was recovered at Springdale, Notre Dame Bay. After examining the creatures, Dr. Aldrich reported, "One unexpected result of these dissections has been the discovery of the world's largest nerve axon or nerve fibre." He added, "None showed signs of reproductive maturity and none had food in its digestive tracts."

A live giant squid was captured by a Spanish fishing vessel. The following item appeared in the *Atlantic Advocate*, November 1970:

A thirty-three foot squid, taken alive by a Spanish trawler off the coast of Newfoundland, has been brought to St. John's for examination by scientists. The huge squid was caught in late September, and according to Dr. Frederick Aldrich, director of the Memorial University Marine Sciences Research Lab, it's the largest of seven that he has examined in the past ten years.

The Spanish fishermen took the monstrous oddity alive, but it was dead by the time it reached port in Newfoundland. Up to this point, the largest was a twenty-nine and one half foot squid caught off northern Newfoundland in 1964.

There are many different species of giant squid, no fewer than four of these have been found in Newfoundland waters, and forty-seven species in waters around Scotland. Some may be larger than others. The one that attacked Tom Piccott was over 1000 pounds. Those caught since the 1960s have been much smaller, some weighed 350 pounds.

MUN
The late Dr. Fred Aldrick of Memorial University, a world
leading authority on the *giant squid* examining the creature
at the Marine Sciences Laboratory of MUN which is located
at Torbay, north of St. John's, NL.

The eating of squid is a common practice throughout
Newfoundland, and the assumption was that giant squid would
taste no different than the ordinary squid. In 1974, when a party of
scientists in St. John's tasted giant squid for the first time, it led to
an important scientific discovery. Dr. Clyde Roper of the
Smithsonian Institute and several other scientists were guests at
the home of Dr. Chung Cheng Lu in St. John's when Dr. Roper
raised a question about how a cooked giant squid would taste.

Dr. Cheng Lu had some pieces of a giant squid stored in his
freezer, and offered to have it prepared and cooked for the gather-
ing. It was cut into frying pieces, some seasoning was added and it
was then pan-fried. Each person's response after tasting the exotic

dish was to show a sour face and utter the word "Awful!"

Instead of depositing the 'lot' in a garbage bin, the group of scientists wondered why the taste would be so different than that of a regular squid. To satisfy their curiosity the cooked squid was examined in a lab and an important discovery was made. The examination revealed that instead of the salt solution found in the tissue of many squid species and other animals the giant squid had in its flesh 'ammonium chloride.' Ammonium Chloride is lighter than salt water and makes the giant squid more buoyant and easier to control its depth. The giant squid attracts fewer scavengers because of its content of this chemical.

If by now you are a little tired, of reading about 'Giant Squid' attacking and eating people, perhaps you might enjoy turning the table on these creatures, and eating some squid. If so, I am told, the following is a remarkably good recipe. It's called:

Squid Fritters with Applesauce.
1 lb. cleaned squid tubes, fresh or thawed.
flour
cooking oil

Batter:
1/2 cup flour
1 egg, dash salt & pepper
1/2 cup water

Applesauce:
1 tsp. cornstarch
2 tbsp. cold water
1-cup applesauce
tsp. grated lemon peel
1/2 tsp. sugar
2 tbs. ketchup

Blend cornstarch with water. Add to applesauce and cook two minutes. Stir in lemon peel, sugar and catsup. Serve hot.

Simmer squid in two cups boiling salted water one hour or

pressure cook five minutes. Drain, cut squid in quarters. Dry well. Combine batter ingredients and blend until smooth. Heat oil to 375° F. Dip squid in flour then in batter. Deep-fry 4 pieces at a time, about 5 minutes until golden brown. Drain well. Serve with applesauce.

Chapter 4

Trains, Buses and Horses

Stranded on Train in Winter Storm

For seventeen days during the winter of 1903, the attention of Newfoundlanders was focused on the plight of one hundred passengers stranded in a train, in almost daily blizzard conditions at the Gaff Topsails, an area of hills in western Newfoundland described by nineteenth century surveyors as the Himalayas of Newfoundland.

The Reid Newfoundland Railway express train left St. John's on February 17, 1903 for a cross-country trip during which passengers were dropped off and new passengers taken on at communities along the way. The train remained on schedule until February 23 when it neared the Gaff Topsails. Blizzard conditions had deposited fifteen to twenty-three-foot-high drifts along the railway line, which forced the train to a complete stop. The telegraph operator aboard the express sent a message to St. John's that the train, which now had one hundred passengers aboard, was stranded at Kitty's Brook near the Gaff Topsails, just east of Sandy Lake.

In the days that followed, newspaper reports told of the plight of those stranded on the train and the constant daily battle with snow, high winds and frost. The frost became so severe that rescue teams sent by the Railway Company could work only short shifts or suffer frostbite. Conditions deteriorated to the point that even when extra money was offered workers, it was difficult to get anyone to work outside in the terrible freezing conditions.

On the train, every effort was made to make passengers as comfortable as possible. Food was provided at no cost, and passengers and crew joined together to cut and retrieve wood to burn and keep the train warm for all concerned.

Snow continued to fall for fifteen days with temperatures ranging between three and twenty-three degrees below zero. The Railway Company sent out fifty snow fighters (men sent out to rescue trains that were derailed or stranded by winter snowstorms) and a relief train escorted by a rotary-plough train to clear the tracks. The rotary was derailed, and the relief train became stranded in the snow. A major effort was required in order to get the rotary back on the tracks. The rescue train, which had been sent from Bay of

Courtesy City of St. John's
The main Newfoundland Railway Terminal in 1900 was at Fort William in the east end of St. John's. The tracks ran along Empire Ave to the eastern Terminal. This photograph shows the Railway Station at Fort William.

Islands, exhausted its thirty tons of coal after just one day of battling conditions at the Gaff Topsails.

Some passengers decided to take the risk of walking through the storm to nearby villages. William Coombs of Brig Bay on the northern peninsula was among those who left the train. Two weeks later, he walked into his home at Brig Bay to the amazement of friends and relatives. Coombs had walked 250 miles, stopping at Bonne Bay and Deer Lake to rest. The factor that contributed to William Coombs' success was that he was an experienced outdoorsman familiar with the area.

Eventually, with the help of snow fighters, the train managed to move slowly, inch by inch, and arrived at Port aux Basques on March 10. The ordeal had taken fifteen days. The train's engineer commented to a reporter, "We met the devil and we beat him."

A similar incident took place during February-March of 1905. In that instance, the train took five weeks to travel from Port aux Basques to St. John's. The train's crew was forced to resort to tearing up the railway ties behind them to use as fuel to keep the train moving. This was not the last time this practice was used to keep a train moving in desperate conditions.

In 1959, 700 train passengers were stranded in two trains at Clarenville when a two-day blizzard struck. A pregnant woman among the passengers decided not to wait out the storm. She set out on foot and walked seven miles to the nearest hospital where she gave birth to a seven pound, two ounce baby boy.

Burning Train

Trains going off the tracks were not an unusual occurrence, but the derailment of the Number 1 Express on February 5, 1917 was one to be remembered in the history of the Newfoundland Railway. Thirty-five passengers traveling in the 'Colonist' car (second-class car) became trapped as it rolled over a bank and burst into flames. By the time the ordeal ended eight passengers were dead.

The Number 1 Express had left St. John's on Sunday, February 4, 1917, with Engine 115 driven by Engineer Webber, with Conductor Lush in charge of the train. About 3:00 a.m. on February

A train accident on the Newfoundland Railway line sometime in the 1930's.

5, while most passengers and crew slept, the coupling connecting the tinder car[1] to the engine severed its connection, giving the train a heavy jolt. Without the weight of the tinder attached to the train, the two foremost cars, along with the tinder, were forced over the side of the track.

In the 'Colonist' car the lamps exploded, spreading burning kerosene throughout the enclosure, quickly igniting all the passengers' clothing, as the coach itself rolled down the embankment. The roar of Engine 115 and the clickety-click of the train as it chugged along on the crisp winter's night was now replaced with the horrible screams of human beings being incinerated.

W. Thistle and L. Knight, the mail clerks, narrowly escaped death while the train was being derailed. As was the custom on leaving Gambo, which is forty miles east of Glenwood, Thistle lay down for a few hours rest while Knight kept watch. After completing some unfinished work, Knight put out one of the two lamps and turned the other down on low. This move was a major factor in saving both their lives.

When the mail car was thrown from the tracks, the light went out, and the oil from the lamps scattered all over the car and saturated their clothing. Thistle was sleeping in the only berth, close to where Knight was standing near the bags of mail piled up in the west end of the car. Both men were thrown across the bags of mail, which saved them from receiving severe injuries. After extricating themselves from beneath the mail, they grabbed the loose registered letters and escaped through the top of the car, which was badly broken apart. The two mail clerks escaped without a scratch.

Among the passengers were R.G. Reid, whose family owned the Railway, and Dr. Jones from Avondale. Reid launched an immediate effort to rescue those trapped in the Colonist car. The mail clerks, Knight and Thistle along with several other train workers and some passengers, joined him. They succeeded in saving all but eight of the trapped passengers. Dr. Jones provided medical attention to the injured.

1. The tinder car was directly behind the engine and carried the coal to fuel the train.

When news of the ordeal reached St. John's, the sad tale of Mr. and Mrs. Moses Rodway of Mussel Harbour Arm, Placentia Bay was revealed in city newspapers. Rodway was the first to escape after the accident and was clearing the way for his wife to follow. She had collapsed and was unable to hear the cries of her husband directing her to the only escape route, which was through a window near the door.

When she failed to respond, Rodway made an effort to rescue her. He plunged back into the flaming car and reached the side of his wife. She was already dead. While trying to drag her from the train he, too, was overcome with smoke and died. Rescue workers arriving at the scene found Moses Rodway with his arms wrapped around his dead wife.

The remains of the Rodways were placed in a small box and brought to Placentia Junction where undertaker Andy Carnell from St. John's placed them in a casket.

Newspapers described the accident of February 5, 1917, as, "The worst railway accident in the history of the country. Derailments have been only too common, but they have usually been attended by such trifling effects as to blind many to the terrible elements of danger they contain."

Train Tales from the Barrelman

This history of the Newfoundland Railway is filled with stories of adventure that took place on the trains. The adventure experienced by William Pike was not on the train, but trapped in the plough at the front of an engine, steaming along in freezing temperatures.

The following item, collected by Joseph R. Smallwood and used in his Barrelman broadcast, tells of the endurance of train workers in fighting winter storms to keep the trains operating. Smallwood told radio listeners to his program:

There aren't many people who don't appreciate a free ride on a train, but there are few, if any, who would like the kind of free ride that Mr. William Pike of Spruce Brook on the West Coast once had. Around five or six o'clock of this particular day in March, he was walking along the railway track towards the station. 'Twas snowing and blowing at the time and he didn't hear the train coming along, an express, until the push–plow caught him up suddenly from behind and began to carry him along. Fortunately, it was only four or five hundred yards from the railway station – and fortunate again that it wasn't a paper train from Corner Brook to Port aux Basques, because in that case the train mightn't stop for two or three hours, by which time he'd be frozen to death or pretty close to it. That's all that worried him – if 'twas the express okay, she'd stop; if a paper train, goodnight! Except for the breaking of a small bone in his ankle, Mr. Pike was none the worse for his unwanted free ride. The experience taught him to watch more carefully when walking along the railway track in a snowstorm.

Another Barrelman story of the old Newfoundland Railway involved the remarkable endurance of the men whose job was described as snow fighters. These were the men sent out to rescue trains stranded by winter storms. He told listeners:

These Newfoundlanders certainly needed out-of-the-ordinary powers of endurance. In the winter of 1922 there occurred a train wreck near the Gaff Topsails. A section man at Millertown Junction was a native of George's Brook, Trinity Bay, named Charles Ellis. 'Twas a Saturday night, and having gone to bed at eleven, he was aroused at midnight to join a gang of men being sent off on a snow fighting job and to the train wreck – it was an engine and a snowplow off the track. The eight of them together with the train-crew finally succeeded in getting engine and plow back on the track, and then they all left on the train for Humbermouth, where they arrived at half-past twelve the next day, Sunday. At four o'clock that same afternoon they were ordered back to Howley snow-fighting their way, and no sooner had they arrived at Howley when they got word of another wreck at Gaff Topsail, so on to Gaff Topsail they had to go without a moment's delay. What with fighting their way through the snow to get to Gaff Topsails, and a very difficult job after they got there, 'twas Thursday morning before they cleaned up the wreck and got the other engine and plow back on the track. It was 9:00 a.m. Friday before the eight of them arrived back at Millertown Junction, where after a rest of a mere hour they all turned again to work along their two sections east and west of there until six o'clock that afternoon-making it six nights and seven days of continuous work snow-fighting in the frosty winter with no, or very little, sleep. Truly, a remarkable performance.

Stormbound

During April 1935, a passenger train of the Reid Newfoundland Railway encountered a major wind and snowstorm that trapped it in heavy snow with seventy-five passengers, in addition to the train's crew, for ninety-six hours. The *Evening Telegram* headline to the story read "*96 Hours Stormbound on Roof of Country.*"

Among the passengers who endured the ordeal in the area on Newfoundland's west coast known as the Gaff Topsails, was Reverend Ira Curtis, minister of the George Street United Church in St. John's. Reverend Curtis was returning to St. John's from Toronto and was joined in Nova Scotia by Dr. H. Cowperthwaite, who was returning to the capital city from a visit to the United States.

Describing the ordeal, Reverend Curtis told reporters that they had left Port aux Basques at 5:00 a.m. on Wednesday, April 3. By evening they were in the midst of a raging wind and snowstorm that forced the train to come to a complete halt at the Gaff Topsails.

He said:

A piercing north west wind, driving snow, and hard ground drift were the conditions on the summit, and it was utterly hopeless for the trainmen to work from the outside. The conditions were equally as bad on Thursday as on the previous evening, and generally the cuts filled in with snow to a depth of fourteen feet. Those in charge of the rotary[2] ahead found it difficult to do anything while the drifts prevailed, and when a start was made in this direction, the rotary unfortunately broke down and had to be replaced by another from Bishop's Falls, which prolonged the delay.

All the passengers cooperated with the train crew in making the best of the situation and there was an ample supply of food available throughout the ordeal. Reverend Curtis explained:

During the time the train was stalled, the passengers were made as comfortable as possible by the train crew, and a word of praise is due the conductor, stewards and crew for their excellent service. There was a shortage of certain foodstuffs on board, but these were replenished when the rotary arrived from Bishop's Falls. There was a sufficient supply of coal at the Gaff Topsails for the locomotive, while fresh water was obtained at Wolf Brook, a short distance from the stranded train.

According to the *Evening Telegram* report, during the four days stranded, the passengers exercised themselves in the open air when conditions permitted. Passengers and crew took short walks. These were limited to ten-minute durations due to severity of the weather.

Boy Trapped on Railway Tracks

A young boy named Lilly, from Petries Crossing, had an adventure with the *Newfie Bullet* in January 1947, during which his presence of mind and quick thinking saved his life.

The boy had taken his two-dog sled-team for a ride over the railway tracks. The rotary train had cleared the tracks, leaving a

---

2. An attachment to the front of the engine that cut through snow.

canyon of snow twelve feet high on either side. The boy was enjoying his winter sleigh ride when a loud rumbling sound in the distance startled him. He brought the dog team to a quick stop when
he looked towards a curve in the distance and saw a train speeding
down upon him.

Trapped between two walls of snow and unable to turn around
and outrun the train, the boy made a choice that saved his life. He
had no time to climb the banks of snow, instead, he dived head-
first into a side snow bank and kept burrowing in using his hands
as the train roared by within inches of his feet. Young Lilly had
succeeded in saving himself. Unfortunately, the two dogs were
run over by the train and died immediately, and his sled was
demolished.

Lilly made it safely to his home, shaken badly and saddened
by the loss of his dogs, but thankful that he had survived such a
narrow escape from death.

Immortalized Gaff Topsails

Isaiah Cole of Grand Falls wrote many poems and songs during the 1940s, most of which were published in the various
Newfoundland newspapers which featured local writers. One,
which was popular in 1947-1950, was *The Topsails*. It told the
story of the terrible snowstorms that stranded the *Newfie Express*
so frequently at the Gaff Topsails. The following is part of that
song, which was sung to the tune of *On Top of Old Smokey*.

Stuck on the Topsails, surrounded by snow,
This is the story we hear, as you know,
The train at a standstill, with passengers and crew,
Sleeping or talking – what else could they do.

Stuck on the Topsails, you might as well grin
As you wait for your letter, 'cause the train is not in.
Go to the Post Office and here's what they say:
"The train's on the Topsails, there's no mail today."

Stuck on the Topsails, "It's wicked," said Jim.
"Sure is," old Tom answered, "it is pretty grim.
I remember one winter, I was stuck there three days,
With nothing but snowdrifts at which I might gaze."

Stuck on the Topsails, the snow piled so high
On both sides of the railway like mountains–oh my!
The train can't continue her journey for days,
And our mail then is hung up owing to the delays.

Stuck on the Topsails – what a place to be stuck!
And if you're a traveler, well, that's your hard luck,
To be stalled on the Topsails, but, friend, never mind,
The train will leave sometime the Topsails behind.

The Great Boat and Train Race

One of the most interesting cross-country races in Newfoundland's history took place in June 1916. The race involved a contest between the *Newfoundland Express* and the sealing vessel *Sagonia* from Port aux Basques to St. John's. The officers and crew of the *Sagonia* while socializing with the Engineer and crew of the *Newfoundland Express* at Port aux Basques, argued that their ship could travel from Port aux Basques to St. John's a lot faster than the railway train. The railway men strongly disagreed with the seamen who in response challenged them to a cross-country race. The railway men accepted the challenge and rules were drawn up for the race. Because the participants were scheduled to leave hours apart, it was agreed that the winner would be determined by the time it took to travel from Port aux Basques to St. John's. The *Express* began its cross-country trip at 1 p.m. on Friday, June 9 and arrived in St. John's next day at 7:30 p.m. The total traveling time for the *Express* was 30 1/2 hours. The *Sagonia* left a few hours after the *Express*, and arrived 2:50 a.m. on Sunday recording a travel time of 33 1/2 hours. The clear winner of this unique cross-country race was the *Newfoundland Express*. By the 1940s the speed of the

Newfoundland Express became a public issue as the following reference shows.

Hollywood and the Newfoundland Express

The *Newfoundland Express* was made famous internationally during February 1943 when Joan Blondell, one of Hollywood's top stars of the 1940s, sang a humorous song entitled *The Newfoundland Express* on the radio show *Command Performance*. The performance took place at Carnegie Hall in New York City and was meant to bolster the morale of US Troops around the world.

Carter/Fitzgerald Photography

Joan Blondell playing pool during her visit to St. John's.

Her performance drew many letters from irate Newfoundlanders who cursed the actress and her family, claiming she was poking fun at Newfoundland and Newfoundlanders.

This song referred to the Express as the "Newphie Bullett" [sic] and the name stuck.[3] Although the song's composer is unknown, it is most likely that Blondell herself, or someone traveling cross-country with her on the Newfoundland Railway during her visit to

3. Just where the term "Newfie" came from is not certain. It is believed it was first used by American soldiers arriving in St. John's in 1941. At the time strong Jamaican Rum was being bottled in St. John's and labeled as "Screech." The Americans began calling the product "Newfie Screech" and it is still called that today.

Newfoundland in October 1942, composed the lyrics and music. In Newfoundland newspapers and publications current at the time, there is no mention of the song being known before its broadcast in the United States during February 1943. On August 10, 1943 Private Albert Gaudet of the Royal Canadian Army recorded the Canadian version of the *Newfoundland Express* at a studio in Halifax, Nova Scotia.

Joan Blondell was the first major movie star to visit Newfoundland. She led a USO Traveling Show Troupe and arrived in St. John's on the *Newfoundland Express* on Thursday, October 8, 1942, following a visit to Harmon Air Force Base on Newfoundland's west coast.[4] While in St. John's she visited troops at Fort Pepperrell and Signal Hill, and gave performances for American and Canadian Forces, as well as members of the Royal Newfoundland Regiment. On October 10 she performed on a USO all-soldiers radio show.

During her visit, she heard an old Newfoundland saying "Stay where you're to 'till I come where you're at," which she found charming and began using when addressing an audience. She used the phrase when introducing the *Newfoundland Express* song on *Command Performance*. The actress was shocked and taken by surprise over some of the negative mail she received from Newfoundlanders in response to her radio appearance. From her Hollywood mansion at 7919 Selma Avenue she wrote the following letter to the *Evening Telegram*, which was published on March 23, 1943.

> *Dear Sir,*
> *A few weeks ago I received some extremely vitriolic and blasphemous letters from anonymous Newfoundlanders. These letters criticized and even cursed me, my family and my career. All this because of a Command Performance I did for the men of our armed forces, a radio program on which I worked very hard to*

---

4. Early in 1942 the United States Army extended the branch of the Newfoundland Railway from Stephenville Crossing to Harmon.

*make gay and to afford a few laughs for our over-seas lis-
teners. That it was not taken by all in that spirit was amazing and inconceivable to me. I put the letters aside mut-
tering wryly that in other countries, as well as in the United
States, there are always those unfortunate cranks who
don't like "nothin' nor nobody."*

*But I am now thoroughly flabbergasted, I returned
home today from a long tour of the army camps in this
country to find my desk literally tipping with indignant
protestations, vicious condemnations and rousing ill-wish-
es toward my health and future. In my heart I refuse to
believe that the true spirit of the Newfoundlanders I had the
pleasure to know is behind such a petty onslaught upon a
person whose every thought and effort since the beginning
of the war has been to bring a few moments of cheer to
those who are giving so much for us.*

*For the Newfoundlanders who are outraged, may I say
this: I was born in Brooklyn. I would be bent and gray and
twisted if I shuddered and condemned those responsible for
the endless Brooklyn gags. We Brooklynites have heard
them and laughed at them since Brooklyn was born. When
on this "outrageous" radio program, I sang the*
Newfoundland Express[5], *I also said, "And now to all you
boys from Texas, the lovely Connie Haines will sing* I've
Got a Touch of Texas in My Heart. *The lyrics are as follows:*

> *Got a touch of Texas in my talk,*
> *Got too much of Texas in my talk.*
> *Oh this place will be my ruin,*
> *Ki Ki Yippin' and Wa-Hoofn',*

---

5. Although several different songs entitled "The Newfoundland Express" have been pre-
served in historical accounts of the Blondell controversy, none of these represent the
Newfoundland Express sung by Joan Blondell. One book reference contains excerpts from
what the author claims is the Blondell version but is actually taken from *A Reply to the
Newfoundland Express*, which was written sometime after the Blondell radio performance.
That song has been included in its entirety in this chapter.

Take me back to New York.
Got a touch of Texas in my hair,
Got too much of Texas in my hair.
Yet the sands from Amarillo
Keep a scratchin' on my pillow–
Take me back to Times Square.
For I've seen every part of every part of
What I'm deep in the heart of–
Got a touch of Texas in my walk,
Got too much of Texas in my walk.
Oh the sage may be bloomin',
But for miles there's nothin' human,
Oh, take me back to New York.

This song is number one hit in the USA, which includes the very large State of Texas. Need I say more?

Surely on radio shows emanating from the States you have heard the comics mimic New York talk. "Dis is Toity-Toid Abenue and Toity-Toid Street. Or that southern drawl, "Howdy y'all, a'hm shore glad to see y'all heah?" Some little girl in Newfoundland at some time said, "Stay where you're to and I'll come where you're at."

If it had not been a charming and quaint way of placing words it would have died on her lips, instead its fame grew and grew until it became important and well worth repeating. Even my babies have relayed it to Public School Number Fourteen in Hollywood. It's likely, in fact, to grace the annals and head the list of our choice phrases.

Aside from all of this, do you think for a split second, that a very American girl whose whole heart and soul is earnestly trying to do her share in the war effort, (and this in spite of the endless days away from her husband and babies and home) would dream of spreading ill will in any land that harbored her soldiers?

My father's definition of a sense of humor is – the ability to laugh at one's self. I have remembered that all my life, and it has helped me across some rough spots. Don't waste time cursing me; rather, let's all lift our voices in prayer to God that the whole world may ring with laughter soon again. Come on, "Newphies",[sic] let's shake – what d'ya say."

Joan Blondell
March 10, 1943

Several prominent Newfoundlanders defended Joan Blondell through letters to the *Evening Telegram*. John G. Higgins, K.C. a WWI veteran and famous Rhodes scholar asked in his letter, "Are we losing our sense of humor?"

Another prominent lawyer, George Ayre, provided the most articulate defense of the actress and utilized a little humor of his own in responding to her critics. He wrote "It is a great pity that our cowardly, anonymous writers did not have to bless instead of curse; but they did not. I am prepared to do it for them, and in my simple humble way say:"

May heaven bless you, Joan Blondell,
Your form and acting both are swell;
Let those who curse you go to —
Joe Batt's Arm.
And there, I bet, they'll do no harm,
Come back and with us long do well,
For we all love you, Joan Blondell.

— G.W.B. Ayre, Liberty Hall, March 25th, 1943. 8 a.m.
sitting on edge of bed while making up fire in
bogie preparatory to having breakfast.

The controversy sparked by Blondell's *Newfoundland Express* inspired a Newfoundlander to write the song, *In Reply to the Newfoundland Express*. It was published in local newspapers and was popular in the 1940s. This song was forgotten by the 1960s

and does not appear in any of the published accounts of the
Blondell controversy that I have reviewed.[6]

In Reply to the Newfoundland Express

Oh, come all ye soldiers, a little while will do;
It's all about a little song that was composed by you;
You came down here to guard our shores, but all you do I
guess,
Is running down our country and the Newfoundland
Express.

Before you step foot on our shores, our trains were neat
and clean;
You could walk into the diner and get a decent meal;
But since you started traveling, everything is in a mess,
And it isn't fit to travel on the Newfoundland Express.

As I was riding on the train a little while ago,
I heard a young man speak in a tone not very low;
The language of that young man, my words cannot express,
T'would nearly make your blood run cold on the
Newfoundland Express.

A pretty lady passenger was seated there close by;
Likewise a handsome soldier, with a twinkle in his eye;
He stepped up close beside her and asked her for a kiss,
She raised her hand and knocked him cold on the
Newfoundland Express.

You speak of a young soldier with a bayonet by his side,
Going back to the USA to wed his promised bride;
He leads her to the altar but little does she guess,
He kissed another bride goodbye on the Newfoundland
Express.

6. A second version with the same title was also written in response to the Canadian version of
the *Newfoundland Express*, and is often presented as the reply to the original Blondell version.

You ridicule our countrymen and pass them with a frown,
You say there goes a Newfie, and try to keep him down;
He may not be so modern, but when put to the test,
I guess he can behave himself on the Newfoundland Express.

Now some of you have sweethearts awaiting over there;
Likewise, an aged mother sitting in an old armchair;
You love them and respect them, and for them you do your best;
So why not treat others, as you treat them, on the Newfoundland Express.

If ever you decide to Heaven for to go,
Don't tie yourself to the railroad track and freeze out in the snow;
St. Peter will give you a ticket to a warmer place, I guess,
And you'll wish you rode a slower train than the Newfoundland Express.

Now to conclude and finish; I hope you won't get sore,
We don't want to insult you, as you did us before;
But before this war is over, if I don't miss my guess,
You'll wish that you were back again on the Newfoundland Express.

Several years later, a parody of this song appeared throughout Newfoundland in which the word "Yanks" was replaced with the word "Canadians." Other words referring to the Americans were removed and several verses were altered. Another song entitled *The Newfoundland Express*, which was flattering to the Newfoundland Railway and was circulated in the province in the mid-1950s, was not the same *Newfoundland Express* sang by Joan Blondell on the *Command Performance* radio show. Writers have also mistakenly put this song forward as the Blondell song of 1943.

On August 10, 1943, a Canadian soldier named Private Albert Gaudet went into a studio at Halifax, Nova Scotia and recorded the Canadian version of *The Newfoundland Express*. Perhaps the only remaining copy of the controversial *Newfoundland Express* is the one stored at the Congressional Library in Washington, D.C.

The Engineer's Dying Child

During the 1940s there was another popular railway-related song, called, *The Engineer's Dying Child*, author unknown.

In a neat little cottage by the railroad track,
A sick child lay and death seemed very near,
He was the only child of a railroad engineer,
Whose duty had called him far away
From his wife and child, so dear,
With hearts broken down in sadness.

They stood in silent prayer,
And with tears in his eyes, he said,
To his wife, "I'll leave two lanterns trimmed,
If our darling's dead then show the red,
If he lives, then show the green."

In a neat little cottage by the railroad track,
Sat a mother with a prayer and a watchful eye,
Saw a gleam of hope in the sick child's eye
As the train went rushing by.
At last, one glance was that engineer's only chance,
But the signal light he had seen,
And his prayer rose up on the midnight air,
Thank God! The light was green.

Wreck of the Number Nine

Long before Joan Morrissey entertained Canadians with her hilarious song, *The CN Bus*, Newfoundlanders were singing the *Wreck of the Number Nine*. The music is the same music used in the

CN Bus song. *Wreck of the Number Nine* was written by Carson Robinson and recorded in 1927 by Vernon Dalhart, one of the first cowboy singers. Others have recorded it since and the lyrics were published in the *Newfoundlander* in the 1940s.

> *On a cold winter night, not a star was in sight,*
> *And the north winds were howling down the line.*
> *With his sweetheart, so dear, stood a brave engineer,*
> *With his order to pull old* Number 9.
> *She kissed him goodbye, with a tear in her eye,*
> *But the joy in his heart he could not hide,*
> *For the whole world seemed bright*
> *When she told him that night,*
> *Tomorrow she'd be his blushing bride.*

> *For the wheels hummed a song as the train rolled along,*
> *And the black smoke came tearing from her stack,*
> *But the headlight agleam, seemed to brighten his dream*
> *Of tomorrow when he'd be coming back.*
> *She sped round the hill and his brave heart stood still,*
> *For a headlight stared him in the face.*
> *Then he whispered a prayer as he threw on the air,*
> *For he knew this would be his final race.*

> *In the wreck he was found, lying there on the ground,*
> *They asked him to raise his weary head.*
> *As his breath slowly went, this message he sent*
> *To the maiden he thought he would wed:*
> *"There's a little white home, I've bought for our own,*
> *When I dreamed we'd be happy some day,*
> *But I leave it to you, for I know you'll be true*
> *Till we meet at the Golden Gates, Goodbye."*

Historic Note: The first locomotive engine ever built in Newfoundland was given the finishing touches on the 30th of August 1911 in the Reid, Newfoundland Company's machine shops here in St. John's. Her number was one hundred and eleven. Mr. R.G. Reid, in the presence of a large number of employees and other spectators, set it in motion for the first time.

On the second of September she made her first run out as far as the head of Conception Bay. Mr. Reid took the throttle on the round trip and he got her up to thirty-five miles per hour several times on the run. Conductor for the special trip was Mr. Stephen Howlett.

– The Newfoundlander, **March 1951**

On the Buses

One need not have been on a boat, train or plane to experience fear and adventure. There were many stories of narrow escapes from the old Golden Arrow buses that operated in the city of St. John's during the 1940s.

On October 26, 1946 the *Evening Telegram* reported:

> *A front to rear collision involving two Golden Arrow buses on Water Street Tuesday afternoon sent four people to the General Hospital suffering from minor injuries and slight cases of shock and resulted in extensive damage to both vehicles.*

According to the story, the accident might have been far more serious had it not been for the decision of the bus driver of West Loop No. 107 to deliberately ram the back of the Hospital Route No. 203. The driver of No. 107 struggled to keep control of his bus as its speed increased going down Prescott Street after its brakes had failed. At the Water Street intersection the driver quickly turned the bus in hopes he could decrease its speed and gain control. He prayed that there would be no traffic or pedestrians in the street during the crisis on No. 107. When he turned, he could see that there was a car on the north side of the street and the Hospital route bus was stopped near the eastern side of Job's Cove. He had to make an instant decision. If he ran it in over the sidewalk at Job's Cove, he would risk injuring or killing one of many pedestrians in that area. A second choice, just as fraught with danger, was to go down Job's

Courtesy City of St. John's
Old St. John's bus going east on Water Street in pre-Confederation era.

Cove, which had a very steep grade, to the water's edge. He decided to ram the back of the Hospital route bus and hope for the best.

Only four people had to be taken to hospital for treatment of non-life-threatening injuries. Almost all the passengers on the 107 were in shock and private cars and taxis were engaged to take them to their homes. No. 203, although having damage to the rear, was able to continue on its route for the rest of the shift. Passengers in the bus were saved from being injured with flying glass by the new shatterproof windows that had been installed in the buses.

No. 107 was considerably damaged and had to be towed from the scene. The *Telegram* noted, "Eyewitnesses agreed that the accident was unavoidable, and in choosing to hit the other bus the driver of 107 made the wisest choice under the circumstances."

Out of Control: Mike Cahill, driver of a Golden Arrow passenger bus in St. John's during the 1940s, found himself with a bus with no brakes, full of passengers and speeding down Long's Hill. Only nerves of steel and cool-headed thinking stood between him and a major tragedy.

Cahill had just driven across LeMarchant Road where he had picked up many passengers, most of whom were heading for Bingo

at the BIS on Queen's Road. At the Grace Hospital a woman passenger got on board and took the seat in front of the bus near the
driver. Old time buses had a double seat opposite, but facing the
driver and adjacent to the front window.

The St. John's Auto Works was a popular garage in old St. John's.

The ride was uneventful until after dropping off a passenger at
the top of Long's Hill opposite Mickey Duggan's Barber Shop.
When Cahill pulled away from the stop to continue down hill, he
placed his foot on the brake to control the speed during the descent
and was startled to find the brakes had given out. Pumping the
brakes proved to be a wasted effort. While the bus picked up speed,
Cahill tried to slow it down by shifting into low gear, but this move
also failed. The speed had reduced a little but the bus was still out
of control.

Only the lady in that front seat was aware of the situation and
she was frozen with fear. Mr. Cahill, fearing what might happen
when he reached the intersection at Long's Hill, began flashing his

Courtesy of City of St. John's Archives
Prior to Confederation automobiles, busses and horses shared Water Street. This photograph shows Water Street east of McBride's Hill.

lights and blowing the horn. Passengers, unaware of the loss of brakes, began shouting for the driver to slow down.

Fortunately, there was no traffic at the intersection, and the bus traveled across Queen's Road and down the slope by Gower Street Church. Cahill thought to himself that if he could turn the bus at the Gower Street intersection and then up Church Hill until she slowed down he might be able to bring her to a slow crash and minimize injuries.

To his surprise, he was able to make the turn, and once again was able to go onto Church Hill. The bus was going fast enough to make it up Church Hill where Cahill turned right onto Queen's Road with the bus coming to a stop in front of the BIS.

While he took a deep breath and thanked God for delivering the bus from what seemed to be a certain tragedy, a woman stormed up from the back of the bus and struck him in the head with her hand. She scolded him for reckless driving and promised to contact the manager of the bus company to make sure he got fired.

At this point, the lady in the seat opposite Cahill told the angry passenger that the brakes had given out on the top of Long's Hill, and if the driver had not struggled to control the bus, they would have all likely been killed. The angry woman quickly apologized to the driver and was one of several on the bus that night who, in a letter to the bus company manager, lavished praise upon the driver's handling of the crisis.

Oldtime Activities on Quidi Vidi Lake

Quidi Vidi was better utilized for recreation in nineteenth and early twentieth century St. John's than in modern times. Not only was the pond the home of the St. John's Regatta, it could also boast of skating competitions, ice-sailboat racing and the mid-winter Derby Day Horse-Racing which was usually held on St. Paddy's Day.

The *Evening Telegram* of February 1894 reported that during February, the ice was good at Kitty Vitty (Quidi Vidi) and, "... Horses with catamarans and sleighs, double and single attached, and driven by expert horsemen, careened up and down the pond preparing for the great race to come off by & bye." (Reference is to St. Paddy's Day Racehorse Derby).

By Derby Day, excitement throughout St. John's over the horse races was running high and over 4000 people turned up for the event. The crowd would have been larger, but for a winter storm that struck shortly after noon and discouraged participants and fans, particularly from the out-harbors, from making the trip to Quidi Vidi.

The big event got underway on St. Paddy's Day at 2:00 p.m. from the lower end of the pond. The horses ran over a three-quarter mile long course that ended at the head. The first race was exciting and contentious. From the start *Nelly Clyde* and *Harry Mac* ran neck and neck. *Nellie Clyde* edged ahead, but *Harry Mac* gained in a photo-finish ending. Fans insisted that *Harry Mac* had won by a half-length. The judges decided it was a tie. Other horses in the race were *Carrie* and the *Tempest*.

The pony race had to be cancelled and was replaced with a Cabman's Race. The *Evening Telegram* explained:

> *The pony race, which was looked forward to with greater pleasure than the other races, did not come off as*

*anticipated owing to the storm. The out-harbour folk
thought it wiser to stay home than visit Quidi Vidi for the
purpose of earning a barrel of flour or a bag of potatoes.*

Palmeter's horse won the Cabman's Race, with Mat Kelly's
coming in second.

Patrons of Derby Day who wanted to attend the races, but avoid
the chilly and stormy weather, took refuge in Professor Danielle's
Royal Pavilion, which by the Professor's own description, "...was
substantially built and has accommodations for two thousand persons." There were numerous windows in the building from which
patrons could view the Derby.

The Committee that organized the event expressed gratitude to
the Professor and the police for their role in making the event a success. The Professor had leased property upon which he built the
Pavilion. However, J.L. Ross, the owner of the property, harassed
him from the beginning because he felt the Pavilion was taking
business away from him. Ross also operated a hospitality home
from his farm.

The *Evening Telegram* referred to the dispute in its coverage of
the Derby:

> *The spectators and committee of management are
> greatly indebted to Sub-inspector Sullivan and staff for the
> excellent order maintained throughout, and to the Professor
> (Danielle) for the elegant, elaborate and sumptuous spread
> provided at his lakeside mansion (Royal Pavilion). It is
> painful to think that a man of the Professor's go-ahead spir-
> it should be hampered as he is. We are afraid that the owner
> of the ground is doing everything he can to make the
> Professor's enterprise a failure. Even the steps placed for
> us to enter his residence from the lake were removed. Let us
> by all means help the Professor, as he deserves.*

The battle between the Professor and Ross ended with the
Professor disassembling his Pavilion piece by piece and sending it

by train from Fort William to the Octagon Pond where he used the building material to construct his historic Octagon Castle.

The Quidi Vidi Horse Race Tragedy

Excitement was high throughout the city of St. John's on the eve of St. Patrick's Day, March 17, 1944, and with good reason. In addition to the celebrations associated with St. Paddy's Day, people anticipated the revival of the Newfoundland Horsemen's Association classic Annual Horse-racing competitions on Quidi Vidi Lake. The horse races had not been held in eight years, and the revival of the annual event, which dated back to the mid-nineteenth century, was certainly an occasion to celebrate.

On the afternoon of Friday, March 17, one of the largest crowds ever to attend any local horse race gathered at Quidi Vidi Lake to enjoy the event. The ice had been tested, and being three to four feet thick, was considered safe. In fact, the tradition of spectators taking their own horse-drawn wagons or motor vehicles onto the ice was very strong that day. The only area of danger was near the west end of the pond where a strong current from Rennies River enters the lake, and sweeps along to a point opposite the Penitentiary where it weakens. The danger to the public in this area had not escaped the attention of the organizers of the event. A rope was extended across the area to warn pedestrians and drivers to stay away.

Many residents of the Blackhead Road area were at the Lake to support their favourite son, Paddy Viquers. Viquers operated a large general store on Shea Heights, and had registered *Sidney,* his pony, in the Pony Contest. Among the Viquers' supporters were Walter Collins and his wife, in their one and one half ton GMC dump truck, which carried another thirteen people.

In describing the event, the *Daily News* noted, "...there was plenty of class to the trotting experts that showed their wares." The races were scheduled to get underway at 3:15 p.m., but were delayed because the owners of a famous trotter at the time, *Dr. Mac,* was unable to get their entry from Carbonear to Quidi Vidi on time. Consequently only two horses, *Peter Pin* and *Cabot Trail*, both owned by Gus Lawlor, competed in the first race. Four heats had to be run to decide the winner. *Peter Pin* with driver Willis 'Pop' Reid won the first, second and fourth heats, thereby winning first place honours. The driver of *Cabot Trail* was Neddie 'Sonny Boy' Vincent. *Peter Pin* was considered to be one of the fastest horses ever seen locally. *Cabot Trail* was a handsome well-behaved chestnut, and a very fine racer, but was scared by the large crowd.

Excitement grew as the program continued with the Class B Trot or Pace Category. The two horses contesting this race were *My Girlie*, owned by the Club Commodore, and driven by Paddy Murphy, and *Sir Charles* owned by Neville Bugden and driven by Harry Bugden. This race was a hotly contested crowd pleaser. Each horse won two heats, and a fifth heat had to be scheduled to decide the winner. It was a close contest all the way and hard to tell who was in first place. There was loud cheering as *My Girlie* won in a photo-finish ending.

Then it came time for the pony race, which the fans from Shea Heights and Blackhead had been anxiously anticipating. This race had five participants: *Bess* and *Maud*, owned by Broadway Stores Ltd., Carter's Hill; *Sydney*, owned by Paddy Viquers, Blackhead Road; *Queenie* owned by Stan Rose Grocery, Campbell Ave, and *Prince* owned by E. Bellows, Blackler Ave. This contest called for the best two of three heats.

The fans from Blackhead Road cheered loudly as *Sidney* took the second and third heats to win the race. The order of the finish was:

1st - Sidney, driven by Swag Kearsey
2nd - Bess, driven by B. Austin
3rd - Queenie driven by Ron Rose
4th -Maud, driven by J. Halliday
5th - Prince, driven by Ed Bellows

Paddy Viquers truly had the luck of the Irish. He had won *Sidney* in a raffle held by the Jubilee Guild, and the horse was christened *Sidney* by Lady Anderson.

The excitement was such that throughout the races, the large crowd often pushed onto the racecourse, which made the job of officials running the contests very difficult. When the races ended, the

officials were relieved that the behavior of the crowd had not resulted in any injuries.

Several hundred people were still gathered on the lake after the
awards had been presented. Soon they were to witness a horror that
nobody had expected. A danger that had not been noticed was lurk-
ing on the ice. Sometime during the afternoon someone had
removed the rope that kept people and vehicles from the thin-ice
area.

Walter Collins started up his dump truck, and waited until his
friends and neighbours had gotten aboard the vehicle. Seated in the
front of the truck were Walter, his pregnant wife, and their neigh-
bour, Mrs. McGrath. Some of those in the back of the truck were
Mrs. McGrath's son John, Donald Boone, L. Moore, K. Barry, P.
Barry, George Street, Max Warford, Gordon Warford, Eric Larkin,
Wallace Smith, Michael Denine and Thomas Denine. There were
fifteen people in the truck altogether when Walter started it, and
slowly moved towards shore.

It was 4:30 p.m. when the wheels of the truck rolled onto thin
ice at a point opposite the Penitentiary grounds, and about 120 feet
out from Clancy Drive, which skirts the lake on the south side.
Walter Collins had driven the truck from the race course area of the
pond, and was attempting a turn to drive onto Clancy Drive when the
back wheels moved from ice that was several feet thick onto ice that
was just four or five inches in thickness. The crowd in the truck was
recalling the highlights of the day, and, in particular the success of
Viquers' *Sidney*. The ice suddenly broke open and the truck, with its
fifteen occupants, disappeared into ten feet of water. A picture taken
by the Royal Navy shortly after the accident showed only the front
of the vehicle and a headlight still protruding from the water.

Collins immediately reacted as the truck began to submerge,
and he managed to get himself and his wife out of the cab of the
truck. Suddenly, many of those in back were struggling to get out
of the water. Fortunately, there were several police officers nearby.
Constables Pelley, Grandy and Rendell, with the help of several
civilians, swiftly moved into action. They managed to rescue people from the water. The police rescued Eric Larkin, Max Warford

and Gordon Warford, and arranged to have them taken to the General Hospital.

In the panic of the moment, nobody knew exactly how many were in the truck, nor if there was still anyone trapped beneath the ice. The police took charge, and used a rope to tie to the part of the truck that was above water. Joined by some of the people present, they struggled without success to pull the vehicle from the water. They nearly had it out of the water when the rope broke, and the truck slid until the top of the cab was under about four feet of water.

By this time, District Inspectors Walsh and Case had arrived, and they took charge of the rescue effort. A call was placed to the Americans at Fort Pepperrel who immediately responded by sending a tractor and portable crane with some U.S. soldiers under the command of Major C.J. Knudson. It was not until about 11:00 p.m. that they managed to get the truck from the water. The Americans cut away the ice to make an opening to shore, then used chains to connect the truck with the crane on shore, and managed to bring the vehicle to the nearby road.

The only body found was Mrs. Bridget McGrath who was still in her seat in the cab of the truck with her hands folded across her chest. Her glasses were still on, and there was no evidence that she had made any struggle. It was believed that she might have suffered a heart attack brought on by the incident.

By midnight, police had determined that the two Denine boys, Michael and Thomas, and Wallace Smith were still missing. The police searched until after midnight, then called off the operation until early the next morning.

The search was resumed early Saturday with Sgt. King directing Constables Cross, French and Shannahan in trying to recover the bodies of the three youths. Bill Denine, an older brother of Tom and Mike, removed a wooden paling from a fence surrounding a nearby farm and attached a hook to it. When he began using his contraption to search for his brothers, the police told him that he was wasting his time, and should leave the search to them. At 11:00 a.m., the police succeeded in finding the body of thirteen-year-old Wallace Smith. An hour later, Bill had extended the paling and hook beneath the ice in an area not far from where the tragedy had taken place. He felt a resistance, and when he pulled it to the surface, it was the body of his brother Thomas. He got Tom to the surface, and then plunged the hook into the same area and succeeded in recovering the body of his other brother Mike. Thomas Denine was twelve years old and Michael was fourteen years old.

Mrs. Collins suffered a miscarriage during the tragic accident.

Reg Collins, a survivor of the tragedy now living in the Goulds, was able to shed some new light on the cause of the tragedy. Collins was one of the boys in the truck during the tragedy, but was not mentioned in newspapers because he had been taken to the General Hospital. Seventeen-year-old Reg lived on Catherine Street and on the day of the tragedy, was visiting his relatives, the McGrath's, on Shea Heights.

He was one of four youths in the back of Walter McGrath's truck going to the horse races. He revealed that after the event, when Walter was turning his truck around so that he could drive onto Clancy Drive, a group of young fellows from Shea Heights began climbing into the truck to get a ride home.

This added weight, in a dangerous area of the pond, no doubt contributed to the truck going into the water back end first. This was followed by panic, confusion and shouts for help. Once in the icy waters, young Reg kept his cool and looked around him to see what was happening. He noticed the driver had his door open and was trying to pull someone from the cab.

Reg's cousin had grasped his leg and was shouting for help. Reg kept one arm on the solid ice and used his other arm to try and rescue his cousin. Out of nowhere a policeman grabbed Reg and was telling him to let his cousin go. The constable said, "We'll get him next." With the officer's help, the two boys were rescued and taken to a cottage on Clancy Drive next to the Anglican Cemetery.

At the cottage, Reg recalls being embarrassed when told by the lady of the house to, "Strip!" There were three or four other ladies in the house at the time. Although reluctant, he was cold, shivering and anxious to get out of his wet clothing. Once he had dried and was wrapped in warm clothing, he and his cousin were taken to the General Hospital.

Reg, a veteran of the Korean War, is able to talk about the tragedy today with respect for the loss of life, and also with a little humor. He noted that he had a partial plate of four teeth, which he lost in the water while trying to rescue his cousin, and adds, "Whenever I am near Quidi Vidi today, I can just imagine a trout swimming by and looking up from the water flashing my lost teeth!"

Other sources told of a young boy named Joey Yetman, who was also in the back of the truck when it went down. Yetman, who passed away in recent years, kept the memory of the tragedy alive among his own family and friends.

Although horseracing at the pond was popular, like the rowing Regatta, it had its opponents. Because it attracted much gambling and some drinking, there were many who advocated putting an end to it. Others complained that it was cruel to animals to force them to race over the ice-race course.

Iceboat racing also took place at Quidi Vidi, although it was not as well organized as the horse races. The day prior to the horse races, according to the *Telegram*, "Messrs. Bowring's and Harvey's iceboats were out and cut merrily across the ice. One of them ran into a little boy, and the boat being heavier, the boy was hurt considerably, though not seriously.

While skaters, horse-race enthusiasts and ice-sail-boat racers frequented Quidi Vidi during winter, the St. John's harbour also offered a source of winter fun. On the day after the Horse Race Derby, hundreds of young men were on the ice covering the harbour, "...amusing themselves in diverse ways."

The fun included skating, walking and jumping from one ice slab to another, known as 'copying.' Some people fell between the slabs of ice, but were pulled from the water by friends. While all this was going on, others enjoyed themselves shooting 'bull birds.' This practice was condemned by the *Evening Telegram* which described it as, "...the shooting of helpless little birds that were being blown around by the wind."

Chapter 5

Air Adventure and Drama

Hijacked – The Mary Dohey Story

*A*ir Canada Flight 812 was on a routine flight from Calgary to Toronto on November 12, 1971. The Captain and crew chatted as they carried out their duties, and the passengers were settling in for the several hour trip. Just east of Regina, SK at 5:30 p.m. MST (Mountain Standard Time) something unexpected and terrifying happened on the flight. For the next seven-and-a-half hours, the aircraft zigzagged across the sky between Calgary and Great Falls, Montana. Suddenly, the fate of all those on board was thrust into the hands of Mary Dohey, a stewardess from Newfoundland. Flight 812 was in danger of being blown out of the sky at any moment.

This frightening ordeal started when a young masked man, brandishing a twelve-gauge sawed off shotgun, emerged from a washroom in the first class cabin, and announced that he was hijacking the plane.

'You're kidding!" said John Arpin, the flight's purser, who was standing closest to the hijacker.

Just minutes before, the thirty-one-year-old hijacker, Paul Joseph Cini of Calgary, had mingled among the passengers boarding the plane, without being noticed. Since there was nothing out of the ordinary in his appearance, he blended in well. When the plane was airborne, Cini went into the washroom. Unknown to passengers and crew he had smuggled a 12-gauge shotgun and ten sticks of dynamite onto the plane. Paul Cini had carefully planned the hijacking, including an escape route.

The hijacker sent chills up the spine of John Arpin when he turned the gun on Arpin and shouted, "I'll blow you're f——n head off. I'll show you if I'm kidding."

He then passed a note to Arpin with instructions that it be taken to the flight deck. To further impress the Purser with his determination, Cini pointed his gun at the head of Mary Dohey the Newfoundland flight attendant, and ordered Arpin to move. When Arpin left the cabin, the hijacker opened a bag containing ten sticks of dynamite with two wires attached. He told Mary Dohey to hold one wire in each hand. He warned her that if the wires touched, the bomb would explode.

Captain Vernon Ehman of Montreal read the note, and relayed the message to ground control. Flight 812 had been hijacked and the hijacker was demanding $1,500,000 for the safety of passengers and crew, or else he would set off the dynamite and blast Flight 812 right out of the sky. While the captain discussed strategy with ground control, Arpin was returning to the hijacker. Just before entering the cabin, he heard gunfire.

Later recalling the event he said, "I thought he had blown the stewardess's head off. I came back through the door, and thought I was going to get it too. But then I saw Mary Dohey sitting there.

Luckily for all the hostages, Mary Dohey was more than a flight attendant. She had trained as a psychiatric nurse in Newfoundland, and was able to use her professional skills to calm the hijacker, especially in his several erratic outbursts that had the potential for disaster. She told Arpin that the hijacker had told her to sit down beside him. Just before this, Paul Cini was visibly agitated and was waving his gun around when it accidentally discharged, just missing Dohey's head, and penetrating the wall between the first class section and the cockpit. This turned out to be another break for the hostages because the discharge had damaged only part of the electrical equipment, which was not essential to the operation of the aircraft.

Turning to Mary Dohey, Cini asked, "Are you nervous?"

"A little bit," she replied.

"I'm sorry, lady, to do this to you," the hijacker said.

Mary Dohey was born in an attic on Flower Hill in St. John's in 1933. Her mother passed away when she was three, and Mary grew up in foster homes at St. Bride's and an orphanage in St. John's. In 1951, she entered the nursing program at the old General Hospital, and specialized in psychiatric nursing at the Waterford Hospital before becoming an airline stewardess in 1956. This training proved to be invaluable when she found herself in a life and death situation with this hijacking as it developed 35,000 feet in the air.

Mary Dohey drew the hijacker into a conversation, and held his hand, an action that had a calming affect on him. The two talked about a variety of subjects including their families, the Calgary Stampede and even department stores.

During his conversation with Miss Dohey, Cini, who was using the alias Dennis Monroe, said he was a member of the Irish Republican Army, and planned on giving all the ransom money to the Irish cause. At one point, according to Mr. Arpin, the hijacker's mood changed quickly, and "... he went berserk." The mood swing was prompted by a mix-up in his cigarettes with someone else's, and he accused the crew of trying to dope him. Mary Dohey calmly explained there was no such plan, and the mix-up was a simple mistake. Cini accepted the explanation and he settled down.

Courtesy of City of St. John's Archives
Mary Dohey was born in an attic apartment at 39 Flower Hill. When her mother died her father took her to live at St. Bride's, Placentia Bay.

Meanwhile, the captain followed Cini's instructions. As directed, he had changed course and was flying to Great Falls, Montana. Cini's plan was to refuel the jet and pick up the ransom money there. He would then direct the pilot to take the plane to Regina and release the passengers. From there, the plane was to take a polar route to Ireland, where he would deliver the money to the IRA. (Sean Kenny, then the North American leader of the IRA, later emphatically denied that the hijacker had any connection with the organization.) The plane circled Great Falls Airport for two hours to give authorities time to put the ransom together. It then set down, and in just thirty minutes was again airborne with the bag containing the ransom on board. Several crewmembers counted the money, and discovered the bag contained only $50,000. They kept this information from the hijacker who, surprisingly, had not insisted on confirming the amount.

Once in the air, Mary Dohey again diverted Cini's attention. She remembered that during the earlier conversations Paul Cini had expressed a love for children. Mary used this knowledge to persuade him to release the children and the passengers. He agreed, and sent instructions to the captain to return to Great Falls where the passengers were allowed to leave the aircraft. During this time, the hijacker told Arpin to retrieve a suitcase from the cargo section in ten minutes. Pointing the gun at the back of the neck of Mary Dohey, the hijacker warned Arpin that if he failed to meet this demand, "I will shoot the girl."

Mary Dohey continued to try and calm the hijacker through conversation, but when the ten minutes passed and Arpin had not returned, he told her she was about to die. In an effort to buy a little more time, and believing she would soon be shot, Mary asked Cini if she could turn and face him. He agreed. When she turned around, she was facing directly into the barrel of the 12-gauge shotgun. "Kill me later when all the passengers are off," Mary pleaded.

Fortunately, Arpin entered the cabin with the bag and the tension of the moment was relieved. The hijacker then offered Mary Dohey a chance to leave the aircraft with the others. The steadfast courage shown by the stewardess throughout the hijacking continued. She had observed the hijacker throughout the ordeal, and saw how his mood could unpredictably switch from one of calmness to one of volatility. The stewardess did not want to abandon those left on board to this unpredictable man.

While this drama was unfolding, news outlets were broadcasting reports of the hijacking across Canada and the United States. Millions of people followed the reports, not knowing what was happening on the flight. The media puzzled over the zigzag flight and the fact that it had landed twice at Great Falls.

Once the plane was airborne again, a change in plans by the hijacker gave veteran pilot Captain Vernon Ehman an unexpected opportunity to regain control of Flight 812. What happened over the next few minutes took a lot of courage on the part of the crewmembers involved. Cini had announced that he had a parachute, and instead of taking the plane to Ireland, he was going to take the ransom and jump from the plane. The plane's altitude was at that time was 37,000 feet.

In order to open an emergency exit window Cini had to use both hands. He had earlier indicated that he still controlled the dynamite with the wires concealed in his pocket. Just as he laid down the gun, Captain Ehman, who had left the co-pilot to fly the plane, swiftly grabbed the hijacker by the throat with one hand and tossed the gun aside with the other, but Cini was not easy to subdue.

"He fought like a wild man," Arpin later told reporters.

When Captain Ehman cried out for help, Arpin joined in the struggle. Still, they were unable to subdue the hijacker.

Assistant-Purser, Philippe Bonny grabbed an axe from a nearby wall and struck Cini with its flat side. The hijacker continued to struggle.

"I'll blow you all up," he shouted as he reached for his pocket.

This time Bonny struck harder with the handle of the axe. The battle was suddenly over.

"I think we've killed him," said Arpin.

When the plane was landed, the hijacker was taken to a Calgary hospital and placed under twenty-four-hour guard. Charges of hijacking were brought against him while he lay in a hospital bed. He was later tried, convicted and sentenced to life imprisonment.

In December 1975, five years after the incident, it was announced that Mary Dohey, the captain, Arpin and Bonny were to

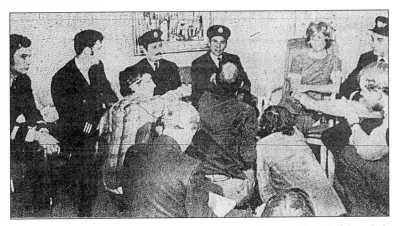

The Captain and crew of the hijacked plane held a news conference at the end of the ordeal. L-R: assistant purser P. R. Bonny; chief officer Jean Belanger; first officer Norm Hagison' captain Vernon Ehman; flight attendant Mary Dohey. The press conference was held in Calgary, Alberta.

be recognized for their heroism. Miss Dohey told reporters she had only one regret, "It was the only time in my life that I had no compassion for another human. When Arpin said he thought they had killed the hijacker, I said, don't expect me to give him first aid, but I've felt badly about that ever since."

When it was announced on December 6, 1975 that Mary Dohey was to receive the Cross of Valour, and that the captain and chief purser would be presented with the Order of Canada, she became very upset because Bonny, who played a major role in ending the drama in the air, had not been included.[1] She communicated her feelings to an official at Government House, Ottawa, with the comment, "If you don't give Philippe an award, I'll give him half my Cross of Valour." When the awards were given in 1976, Philippe Bonny along with the captain and chief purser were presented with the Order of Canada.

During the tense air drama, Mary had silently prayed to God that the passengers and crew be saved. In 1976, she said the real credit for saving everyone that night belongs to God. "The fact that I am still alive is a bonus," she added.

1. Mary Dohey was the first living person to be awarded the Cross of Valor. Two previous awards were given posthumously.

Dive Bombing Over Gander

People in the Gander area were startled on January 19, 1962, to witness a Trans-Canada-Airline plane dive bomb towards the ground then pull up and repeat the dive-bombing action. The plane didn't leave the area, but continued to circle for nearly three hours. Those watching the aircraft maneuvering were not yet aware of the drama playing itself out on TCA Flight 404.

Among the passengers on the flight was Newfoundland's Director of Tourism, Oliver L. Vardy, and St. John's businessman, Graham Mercer. The flight was carrying thirty-four passengers from Gander to St. John's. Less than ten minutes after takeoff the captain was alarmed to discover that the nose-wheel would not go down. Following some discussion with ground control, he decided to remain in the Gander area and try to correct the problem. The craft was a Viscount and had a range of 1700 miles with sufficient fuel to remain in the air for hours. It had a cruising speed of 320 miles per hour and measured eighty-one feet long and had a ninety-three-foot wingspan.

Ground control prepared for an emergency landing and quickly arranged through TCA at Halifax a direct telephone hook-up between the TCA's Maintenance Division at Winnipeg, Manitoba and Flight 404's Captain William Gwyn. Mr. Vardy recalled later that there was no panic among passengers. He said, "When all attempts to free the wheel failed, we were informed that a crash landing would be attempted and we were given instructions on what to do."

While the crew gave passengers instructions on how to prepare for the landing, Captain Gwyn tried desperately to free the nose-wheel. During these efforts the landing gear on the wings of the plane moved into position and locked and Gwyn took the plane to a high altitude and dive-bombed. He followed this dramatic move with bouncing the plane several times on the runway. However, all efforts failed and the nose-wheel remained jammed.

The captain then confided to the crew and then the passengers that the only choice remaining was an emergency landing. He took time to speak with every passenger on the plane to explain how the landing was going to be accomplished. Mr. Vardy said the captain's conversations and the confidence and professionalism of the crew were the factors in avoiding panic among the passengers. On the ground workers were preparing to handle the pending emergency landing. While the passengers were given a briefing on crash procedures, foam was being spread over the runway to provide a smoother slide for the plane and reduce the possibility of fire on impact. Although there was no panic, tension heightened as the plane began its descent. Captain Gwyn lifted the nose of the plane slightly above normal to avoid a sudden nosedive and disaster as it approached the runway.

Flight 404 skidded several hundred feet over the foam-covered runway and after thirty seconds came to a halt. The passengers and crew were quickly evacuated from the aircraft. The captain had ended the near three-hour drama in the skies without any injuries or casualties. When reporters surrounded the passengers as they entered the terminal, they lavished praise upon Captain Gwyn and his crew. The crew included; Captain William Gwyn, First Officer Alex Vance and Stewardesses Solange Normanding and E.C. Gwynne, all of Montreal.

Several passengers were interviewed by the *Evening Telegram* at the airport after the landing. Brenda Purchase of St. John's told the reporter that she thought, "My number was up." The most frightening part for Ms. Purchase was when the plane landed on the foam-covered runway.

Leo Tucker, who was traveling with his wife and two children, described the event as, "a harrowing experience." Frank Murphy, returning to St. John's from Nova Scotia, praised the coolness and professionalism of the captain and crew.

St. John's businessman Gus Winter was accompanied by his seventeen-year-old son. He noted that he first became aware there was a problem with Flight 404 when his son pointed out the aircraft was repeatedly circling the airport. Soon after that, Captain Gwyn announced there was a problem with the plane. Bernard Cook of Bishop's Falls was not frightened during the crisis. However, he added that he did say a prayer as the plane went in for the emergency landing.

This emergency landing marked the first time any such incident occurred in Newfoundland on a TCA flight since the airline began operations in this province in May 1942.

B-17 Lost In Labrador Wilds

With Christmas Day 1948 only a couple of days away, the seven crew members and two passengers of the USAF B-17 on a flight to Goose Bay anticipated celebrating Christmas Day at Goose Air Force Base with family and friends and the traditional hot turkey dinner. However, ground control at Goose Bay received a message that the plane was in trouble and about to make a forced landing. At this point ground control lost contact. Over the next thirty-six hours the B-17 became the center of one of the largest search and rescue efforts undertaken in Labrador up to that time.

The drama began when the engine began to fail, and the pilot, Lieutenant Chester Kearney, decided to make an emergency landing. Before losing contact with the airport he had time to relay a message to Goose Bay that the plane was in trouble and about to make a forced landing. There were tense moments on the plane as it slid across a frozen lake before coming to a stop. There was no loss of life or injuries in the landing operation. Only later did the captain and crew learn they had landed on Lake Dyke, north west of Goose Bay.

One of the most intensive rescue operations ever assembled in the North up to that time swiftly moved into operation and involved the military at Goose Bay, Harmon Field, and Torbay, in Newfoundland as well as Greenland. Lt. Col. E. M. Jones, Director of Operations at Goose Bay was assigned Command over all available search and rescue operations. In less than an hour, Jones had three planes searching the area where last contact was made with the B-17.

Colonel Paul Zartman, Commanding Officer at Goose Bay, described the events of the next thirty-six hours as a "spectacular rescue operation." Several planes were added to the rescue effort and the operation covered one hundred thousand square miles of Labrador territory. All crews were briefed before starting the search by Colonel Jones who told them, "Don't miss a square foot of your assigned areas." Fortunately, weather conditions were fair at the time.

Three planes remained in the air all night and returned to base after dawn at which time other planes were ready to replace them. By dawn on Christmas Eve, thirty thousand square miles had been searched without any sign of the downed aircraft. The search increased and spread out throughout the day. On Christmas Day radio operators at Goose Airport made contact with Lt. Kearney, pilot of the missing B-17. He advised that they had all survived the landing and were doing well. Kearney was unable to identify for searchers the place where they had landed.

By 3:00 p.m. a search plane from Harmon Air Force Base picked up a message from the downed aircraft that stated the stranded men could see the search plane. The radio operator at the crash site directed the search plane toward them.

Having found the stranded men, the challenge remained to keep them alive and in good shape until a rescue party could get to them. In this matter, the search organizers had to deal quickly with a major problem. It could take days to get a search party to them by foot and there was no craft available at Goose Bay that was ski equipped to land on the Lake. To deal with this, Lt. Col. Jones called up the bases at Greenland and Torbay for help. Goose Bay was able to supply a C-47 with ski-equipment that could be attached to a plane to enable it to make a safe landing on the ice-covered lake. They needed special equipment to make this work, so Jones turned to the forces at Torbay Airport for these items. A ground crew at Torbay worked all Christmas night preparing jet-assisted take-off tubes.

Jones next sent out a request to northern bases for an experienced ski-pilot to fly the dangerous mission. He received a reply from Westover Field, Greenland, headquarters of the Atlantic Division that Lt. Col. Emit L. Beaudry, who was an expert pilot, was on his way. The C-47, jet assisted take-off tubes and Beaudry all arrived at Goose Airport just after dawn on December 26. By 2 :00 p.m. the tubes were installed and the plane was on its way to Lake Dyke. Others on the C-47 included; Captain Ervin Werland, co-pilot; First Lt. Robert Shaw, navigator; Lt.-Col. R.C. Kugel, Commanding Officer of the Greenland Base Command and Staff-Sgt. H.G. Horsler, engineer.

By 4:00 p.m. the ski plane sighted the stranded men. They made two passes over the lake checking ice conditions in the area to ensure a safe landing. Beaudry set the plane down as close as possible to the men and the rescue was completed in a very short period. The doors of the C-47 closed, the JATO Tubes started and the C-47 was on its return flight to Goose Bay. One of the two Canadian passengers on the B-17, Mr. J.D. Cleghorn of Montreal told reporters at Goose Bay:

> *After the crash landing we got out of the plane. We had warm clothing and there was some food on the plane. We were very confident we would be found by this search party, which we knew would be in the air looking for us. It wasn't too bad after we saw that first B-17, but we could have stayed for a long time since the country was full of game, we were near fresh water, and there was plenty of wood. We were very thankful that no one was hurt and we got out so quickly.*

While Jones was preparing the rescue effort, search and rescue units in the air dropped food, medical supplies and warm clothing to the stranded men. This assistance enabled the men to spend a more comfortable night even though the temperatures dropped tweny degrees below zero that night.

B-36 on Secret Mission – Crashed Near Clarenville

On March 18, 1953, two USAF B-36 bombers were assigned to carry out a secret mission between the Azores and the United States. An unexpected windstorm interrupted the mission near Maine, and forced one of the bombers 400 miles northward, and off course.

The ten-engine B-36, with twenty-three men on board, found itself in heavy fog over the Clarenville area in eastern Newfoundland. The pilot radioed Gander at about 3:45 a.m. that he was flying at an altitude of 1000 feet. He had no idea that he was on a collision course with 'Lookout Hill,' near Burgoyne's Cove, which was higher than 1000 feet. The bomber struck the hill, and began coming apart. Engines and other debris were scattered. Among those who died in the crash was Brigadier General Richard Ellsworth. Little is known about the mission except that it was to fly from Lagen's Field in the Azores across the Atlantic at an altitude of 500 feet, until reaching the coast of Maine, at which time it was to climb to 44,000 feet and begin its mission.

The heavy fog encountered by the B-36 while crossing the Atlantic prevented the navigator from taking fixes en route. A low-pressure area that was expected to move north in the Atlantic and give winds to carry the aircraft south did not move as expected.

In addition to this, the aircraft steered a few degrees north to counter the expected southward trend. In fact, the winds around the low forced both bombers off course, but the other bomber was fortunate enough to escape the fog and make it safely to a base in the U.S.

Although no one had survived to describe what happened, it is believed the pilot got a quick glimpse of the high hill they were about to hit. Searchers arriving at the crash sight, after considering the pattern of the scattered debris from the plane, suggested the pilot may have turned the plane in an upward direction to avoid crashing, but the maneuver was too late.

While aircraft and helicopters prepared for search and rescue, ground-search parties were already moving into the crash area. Woodcutters from Random Island who reported their find to the RCMP discovered the wreckage the next day. Two search parties of USAF officers were immediately dispatched to the crash scene. The RCMP took another three American officers to the site.

The Americans had strong support from residents living near the crash site. All the men of Burgoyne's Cove, and many from nearby villages took their boats to the area to assist in the search

Courtesy of the Lynch family
The Crash site at Burgoyne's Cove has been preserved and there is a monument at the site.
This photo taken in 2004 shows Colin and Judy Lynch of Paradise, NL standing in front of
one of the engines of the B36.

and rescue effort. It didn't take long for search planes to reach the
area. One of them, a USAF C-47 stationed at Torbay Airport carried two volunteer RCAF paramedics, Corporals Steve Trent and
Joe Couturier, who parachuted to the crash scene.

When interviewed by the *Evening Telegram*, Corporal Trent
described the role played by the paramedics. He said:

> *It was just about six o'clock and close to dark when we
> jumped. The pilot had to fly between the hills, and we were
> about 700 feet up when we left the plane. Joe jumped first
> from the Dak (RCAF designation for the Dak[ota] in which
> they were flown to the scene), but I landed first. I'm heav-
> ier than Joe. We landed in the bush at the edge of a lake,
> about forty feet apart. The trees were about twenty-five feet
> high, and my chute got tangled in them so that my feet
> barely touched the ground. Joe was luckier, he went
> through them, and landed on the ground. This lake was
> about a quarter of a mile from where we'd seen fire, which
> we assumed to be part of the wreck. It was still smoldering*

when we got there, and looked like oil burning. It was eight o'clock, and long since dark by this time, and after we had called out, and got no answer, we put up a shelter for the night.

The next morning the two paramedics returned to the wreckage, and explored the site. Pieces of the B-36 were scattered throughout an area about a mile long. It appeared that the bomber had hit the top of the hill, partly breaking up, and kept on going, scattering debris as it went. Corporal Trent expressed his thoughts on what had happened.

I figured that when the plane hit the hill it somersaulted, crashed down again, and somersaulted again, sliding on down the other side of the hill after hitting the peak. The tail of the plane, the only large piece of it left, was just about at the top of the hill. It was hard work climbing the hill to the wreckage. We'd struggled through the trees for ten minutes or so, climbing almost perpendicularly, and then stopped for a rest. When we got up, we started looking for the bodies. There had been a ground party come in the evening before, and spent the night in the bush, but they were gone when we got up there the next morning. Between us, Joe and I, we found about ten or twelve bodies Thursday morning, before another ground party came in. They were an American officer and several civilians. Before I go any further, let me say that those civilians were the most hospitable people I've ever met. There was nothing they wouldn't do for us. The second night we were in there we spent in a woodsman's cabin, about a half mile from the crash. They're wonderful people. We let the bodies stay where we found them, so that they could be examined in the exact position they lay by an American doctor and coroner. We just covered them over, and marked the spot so that we could find it again.

According to the paramedics the bodies were spread over an area of about four hundred yards long and about twenty yards wide. A few were burned beyond recognition, but most of them were not burned, and these were identified on the spot. The plane crashed about a half mile from the coast near a place called Nut Cove, which was a landing place for woodsmen. Corporal Trent described the terrain:

> *I'd say about that country, it's about the ruggedest I've seen. It's pitted with hills and ravines, rocks and gullies, covered with trees and bush, and in one place in particular the trail ran almost straight up a hill. The reason it took so long in finding all the bodies is that some of the bodies were covered by wreckage, and we wouldn't touch it until the American officers had arrived.*

Trent and Couturier were called upon to parachute into the crash site because there were no other paramedics in the area. An RCAF aircraft took the twenty-three crash victims to Torbay where the Americans arranged to move them to their base at Fort Pepperrell (now Pleasantville). At the base, arrangements were made to send the remains back to the United States for burial.

Throughout the search effort there was plenty of aircraft activity in the crash area. The USAF had search planes and helicopters

Courtesy the Lynch family
This photo taken at the crash site in 2004 shows Colin Lynch and his son Jeff of Paradise, standing inside one of the engines of the B36 and standing near another part of the wreckage.

including a US Navy seaplane, and the RCAF had a Rescue Canso from Torbay. The VOCM's flying newsroom, a small aircraft piloted by Joe Butler sr. flew over the site carrying *Evening Telegram* photographer Ed Ringman, who took the first photographs of the crash site which appeared in newspaper coverage of the tragedy.

A monument has been placed at the crash site, and is accessible to visitors. Neville Webb of St. John's, who visited the area in August 2002 said, "This particular aircraft wreck site is unique because of the size of the aircraft, and the fact that most parts of the aircraft's major structure are still in place."[2]

Colin and Judy Lynch of Paradise, Newfoundland visited the site during July 2004, and were kind enough to provide me with pictures for this story. Judy Lynch explained that the site is not difficult to find, and many people now visit it each year. She said, "To get there, you need to turn east at Clarenville, which will take you to Burgoyne's Cove. There's a dirt road from the Cove to a slate quarry on the shore of Smith Sound. From there you can access the site. There are benches along the trail to rest."

The 515 Air Cadet Squadron, Atlantic Region, has erected a sign at the start of the trail. At the highest point on the ridge is a memorial consisting of a propeller blade taken from the B-36 and a stone memorial with a bronze plaque.

The Rapid City Air Force Base in South Dakota was renamed 'Ellsworth Air Force Base' in honour of General Ellsworth who was killed in the crash.

'Tailend' and The City of New York

At dawn on April 2, 1930, one of the great stars of the Silver Screen, Mary Pickford, was traveling through New York City streets in her chauffeur-driven limousine. With her was her dog 'Tailend,' a Sealyham terrier. Less than twenty-four hours later, a terrified Tailend was running through the woods near the town of Harbour Grace, Newfoundland. On that day, Tailend had been part of an adventure that made headlines around the world. If it had

2. Neville Webb, article appearing on Web site of Goleta Air and Space Museum. www.air-and-space.com

been successful, it would have earned an important place in world aviation history.

Mary Pickford was driving across New York that morning to Roosevelt Airport to bid farewell to John Henry Mears, a close friend and world-famous aviator. Mears had earned worldwide attention for his air adventures. He had circumnavigated the globe in 1923 in twenty-five days, which lowered the previous record by four days. In 1926 that record was broken by pilots Edward Evans and Linton Wells. Mears, accompanied by Captain Charles Collyer, regained the record for the United States in 1928. Flying in his Lockheed Monoplane, the *City of New York* he had circled the globe in less than twenty-four days.

On April 2, 1930, he was out to regain another record for the United States. The *New York Times* reported, "Mears' intention is to make a flight around the globe, his great objective being to beat the twenty-one day record established by the *Graf Zeppelin*, and to bring the speed record back to the United States."

At Roosevelt Airport, Mary Pickford wished Mears success, kissed him, and presented him with Tailend as his mascot for the flight. The *City of New York* left Roosevelt Airport at 8:00 a.m., and its destination was Harbour Grace where it was to start its world adventure. The route to be taken by *The City of New York* from Harbour Grace was as follows: from Harbour Grace to Dublin, Ireland; England; Belgium; Poland; Dantzig; Latvia; Lithuania; Russia; China; Japan; across the Pacific, and back by way of Canada. Mears expected to cross the Atlantic in fourteen hours.

The City of New York, maroon and cream in colour, was described by the *New York Times* as:

> *A combination of strength and beauty, and her lines give every indication of her capability to travel at the speed claimed of 169 miles an hour. With a tailwind she may attain 200 miles. She is fitted with a 425 horsepower Pratt and Whitney Wasp motor, and carries 450 gallons of gasoline, with thirty gallons of mobil oil. About seven pounds of luggage apiece is carried, and food supplies consist of*

thermos bottles of hot coffee, cold water and food concen-
trates. A two-way radio set is also installed, the call letters
being KHIMN. The cabin of the plane is a model of trim-
ness, and there is a place for everything and everything in
its place. Fuel and oil supplies are waiting at Harbour
Grace to replenish the amount required for the ocean
crossing.

Hundreds of people, attracted by news reports of *The City of New York* coming to Harbour Grace, had gathered at the airfield near the town to witness history in the making. Men, women and children stood quietly, scanning the western horizon for the first glimpse of the famous monoplane, as it neared the community.

About four o'clock a message reached the airfield that the monoplane had just passed over LaManche, Newfoundland. At the same time, someone shouted, "There she is!" At first, it appeared as a small dot in the sky, but it got larger and larger until it was easily identified as *The City of New York*. The *Evening Telegram* described the arrival:

It had disappeared behind the bluff, which stands as a landmark at the eastern end of the airport, on the summit of which a cone-shaped signal was flying. The plane, com- ing lower and lower, circled the grounds, and then with a roar of engines, it came with terrific speed landwards from the east, took the ground on the northern side of the run- way somewhat suddenly, and was brought to a stop about midway up the field at 4:25 p.m., less than fifteen minutes after it was sighted.

Herman Archibald of the Airport Committee was near the run- way, and using a megaphone to keep the area clear of spectators. When the Lockheed Vega Monoplane came to a stop, Mr. Archibald was the first person to welcome Mears and Captain Henry James Brown to Newfoundland. Following this, Mears took Tailend in his arms and stepped out of the aircraft. There was a strong presence of international press, and photographers who suddenly rushed forward to greet the two airmen. The two aviators agreed to take questions from the reporters and to describe their flight from New York. At this stage, Tailend appeared to be happy and content.

After interviewing Mr. Mears, the *Evening Telegram* recorded the following description of his flight from New York to Harbour Grace:

> *The time taken from point to point was eight hours and five minutes, and had been without any particular incident. Some fog had been met along the Nova Scotia coast to about Prince Edward Island. The Newfoundland coast was crossed at Cape Ray. Mears said that they had started on the flight in considerable alarm, because of the terrifying accounts they had heard of the fog to be expected over Newfoundland. They were more than delighted to find themselves over a country bathed in glorious sunlight, and presenting a scene of unrivaled beauty, with the streams and lakes gleaming like silver among the hills and forestlands. The most perfect weather conditions were met all the way across the island, and it was possible to pick up the airport without the slightest difficulty.*

Mears was anxious to continue his flight as soon as possible. A mechanic had to check the plane first, it had to be refueled, and supplies for the cross-Atlantic flight had to be stowed properly aboard the aircraft. He expected they would be ready for take off by 2:30 a.m. The Harbour Grace committee warned Mears that it would be dangerous to start the flight before daylight. The two pilots ignored this warning.

At about 4:00 a.m. next day, Brown arranged for cars with their headlights on to park on the western end of the field. On the eastern end of the field he placed flares. The winds were favourable when *The City of New York* took a diagonal direction across the field, which runs from east to west. Tailend was resting on board as the pilot prepared for takeoff.

Just after starting, the pilot experienced trouble. The monoplane was on takeoff down the runway, deviated to the left, and at the southern edge moved about ten feet into the air, then dropped. The engine instantly cut off, but the impetus carried the plane crashing through the brush and over the hedges and rocks for about sixty feet. The plane finally came to a stop, but faced back towards the airport.

As soon as the plane appeared to be out of control, people began rushing to the site to help the occupants. Mears and Brown managed to extricate themselves from the wreckage. The two men appeared to be in shock, and Mears was complaining of an injured shoulder. His first enquiry was about Tailend, who had jumped from the plane at the first opportunity and run away from the airfield. A thorough search of the area by Mears, Brown and the spectators failed to find the little dog that less than twenty-four hours earlier had snuggled up to Mary Pickford in the safety of her limousine.

As news of the crash was telegraphed across North America, an assessment of damages was being carried out. The *Evening Telegram* reported:

> *The tail, from ploughing over the ground was broken off; the propeller blades were bent, six feet was broken off one wing and three feet off the other. The undercarriage was torn off and the body broken just behind the tanks. One wheel was flat, and the other with the struts had been torn off, and flung about twenty feet away. The engine appeared to have been undamaged, while the instruments including the radio were intact. Yesterday, the aviators with Mr. Carlisle, the engineer, who has been at Harbour Grace for some weeks, held a complete survey of the damage, and commenced the work of salvage, with the intention, it is understood, of crating the machine and shipping it to New York.*

Three days after the crash of *The City of New York* a young boy from Harbour Grace playing in the woods found a lost, frightened, but friendly little dog. It was Tailend. The boy brought him home and gave him food and water. The boy's parents arranged to return Tailend to Mears who was delighted to get him back. Mears brought him back to Mary Pickford in New York. While in Newfoundland, Mears and Brown stayed at the Cochrane Hotel in St. John's. The aviators returned to New York on August 9.

On July 6, 1930 a small plane attempting a take-off at Lester's Field, in the Blackmarsh Road area of St. John's, Newfoundland, stalled when in the air, then nose-dived to the ground, and burst into flames upon impact. The single-engine aircraft was quickly reduced to a mass of twisted-metal. Heroic action on the part of several spectators succeeded in saving the pilot, Captain C. S. Wynne-Eyton.

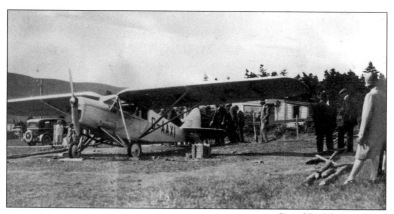

City of St. John's Archives
The Puss Moth at Lester's Field in St. John's.

The aircraft was a De Havilland Puss Moth in which the pilot had hoped to make a trans-Atlantic flight. His schedule included a test flight over St. John's prior to flying to Harbour Grace, where he was to begin the trans-Atlantic adventure.

About 300 spectators were present to witness the Wynne-Eyton flight. When it suddenly turned into disaster, several men rushed to the aircraft, without thought for their own safety, to rescue the pilot. George Symonds was the first to reach the plane. It burst into flames as he approached it. George struggled unsuccessfully to open the cockpit door, which had become jammed when the plane hit the ground. Several others, Don Whiteway, Desmond

Whiteway, Jim Davis, Dan Reardon and John Lundrigan, joined him.

When told by Symonds that the door was jammed, and with flames shooting from the plane, Don Whiteway kicked in the door. The men dragged the pilot from the plane and carried him a safe distance away from it. He was semi-conscious and still clasping the joystick in his hands. Blood was pouring from his mouth and head. A car was brought onto the field, and the victim placed in it. The vehicle then rushed off to the Grace Hospital, located nearby on LeMarchant Road. When the patient arrived at the hospital, he was in shock.

Three doctors: Dr. Harry Roberts, Dr. Blackler and Dr. Fraser attended to him and arranged to have him immediately brought to the operating room. In addition to shock, Wynne-Eyton suffered a severe blow to the mouth when his face had struck part of the front cockpit. His upper lip was almost severed. He also had a cut in the upper gums that went to the bone. His lower teeth were driven so far into his lower lip that surgery was required to correct it.

Mr. Shaw, a mechanic, had checked out the plane before take-off. Mr. Shaw said the aircraft had been positioned in the field in a northwest direction. Shaw had checked the engine and run it for an hour. He concluded that everything was working fine. At 11:17 a.m., it left the ground, reached an altitude of 100 feet, then turned south and dropped to thirty feet. The aircraft struggled to hold this altitude then nose-dived into the ground.

By the time firefighters arrived on the scene, there was nothing but the framework of the plane left. When Mr. Shaw left the field, spectators rushed to the site to collect parts of the plane for souvenirs. The engine and metal work were carted to Lester's Stable on Hamilton Avenue in St. John's.

An investigation revealed that problems with the plane began at takeoff. The engine worked spasmodically after it had been started. There was a problem with the running wheels, and the plane's speed appeared to be no greater than forty miles per hour. Once in the air, the pilot had problems maintaining a safe elevation, and when the plane dipped there was insufficient altitude to allow the pilot to operate the controls in time to prevent the plunge to earth.

Newfoundland – Part of World Aviation History

Newfoundland has played an important role in the history of world air travel. The following chronicles the Atlantic flights made from this province between 1919 and 1938 and includes records of those that disappeared.

City of St. John's Archives
Hawker and Grieve Flight of 1919.

May 18, 1919: In competition for the *London Daily Mail*'s $50,000 prize for the first non-stop air crossing of the Atlantic by a heavier than air machine, Harry C. Hawker and Mackenzie Grieve took off from Mount Pearl, near St. John's, in a 375 h.p. plane. Fourteen and a half hours later, after traveling 1200 miles, they were forced down in the Atlantic near the steamship *Mary*, whose crew rescued them.

An hour after Grieve and Hawker had left, Captain F.P. Raynham and C.W. Morgan, in attempting to take off from Pleasantville, North Side of Quidi Vidi, crashed at the start and had to abandon their cross-Atlantic attempt.

In the same month, the first successful crossing of the Atlantic by air was made by one of the United States Navy's 'Nancy' flying boats from Trepassey. NC–1 dropped into the sea 256 miles from the Azores and was located by a destroyer. NC–3 came down in the water 140 miles from the Azores but reached land under her own power. NC–4 with Lieutenant–Commander A.C. Reed and five others reached Lisbon, a distance of 2,437 miles, with a stop at the Azores.

First Non Stop Flight

June 14, 1919 – The first non–stop crossing of the Atlantic by an aircraft was made by Captain John Alcock and Lieutenant Arthur W. Brown in a Vickers-Vimy plane from Lester's Field to Clifden Ireland, flying 1800 miles in sixteen hours and capturing the *Daily Mail*'s $50,000 prize.

City of St. John's Archives
The Alcock and Brown Flight of 1919.

City of St. John's Archives
The Vickys Vimy aircraft at Lester Field in 1919.

July 4, 1919 – Rear Admiral Kerr, Major T. Grant and Major Brackley left Harbour Grace in the biplane *Atlantic* for Long Island, New York, in the course of an experimental flight before attempting the Atlantic. They abandoned the venture when they damaged their plane in a forced landing in the streets of Parrsboro, Nova Scotia.

August 21, 1924 – The United States Air Corps Round World Fliers, led by Lieutenant Smith, accomplished the first westward crossing of the Atlantic by airplane. They crossed from Reykjavik, Iceland to Ice Tickle, Labrador with stops at Fredeicksdel and Ivigtut, a distance of 1520 miles, in the course of a world flight carried out in a leisurely 175 days.

May 8, 1927 – Disaster marred the attempt by two French airmen, Captain Charles Nungesser and Francois Coli, who left Paris in the plane *White Bird* on a non–stop flight to New York. Although they were reported "seen" in various parts of Newfoundland and Labrador, no trace of them was ever found by searchers.

First Solo New York to Paris

May 20, 1927– Colonel Charles A. Lindbergh, who made the first non–stop solo crossing by plane from New York to Paris in his famous *Spirit of St. Louis* in 33 hours 29 _ minutes, is recorded here because he flew over St. John's and set his course from Signal Hill. In the movie about the Lindbergh flight entitled 'The Spirit of St. Louis', the scene of his flying over St. John's and out over Signal Hill is recreated.

May 23, 1927– Italian aviator Francesco de Pinedo, with Carlo del Pretti and Vitrole Zachetti, flew the *Santa Maria* from Trepassey to within 160 miles of the Azores, where he was forced down. He returned later at the same location and continued the flight to Portugal.

August 6, 1927– Round the world fliers William F. Schlee and William Brock flew from Harbour Grace to Croydon, England in their plane, *Pride of Detroit*. They covered the 2350-mile trip in 32 hours 21 minutes, while on their way to Japan.

September 6, 1927– Lloyd Bertaud, James De Witt Hill and Philip Payne attempted a flight from Old Orchard, Maine, non-stop to Rome in their plane *Old Glory*. They came down in the Atlantic. On September 12, the S.S. *Kyle* of Newfoundland found the wreckage of the plane, but no trace of the fliers, off Capt Race.

September 7, 1927– Captain Terry Tully and Lieutenant James W. Metcalf departed from Harbour Grace for England in their plane the *Sir John Carling*. They were never heard from again.

The Royal Windsor arrived at Harbour Grace the same week. Her two pilots abandoned their Atlantic flight after learning of the disappearance of the *Sir John Carling*.

First Woman to Cross Atlantic

June 17, 1928–Flying from Trepassey, NL to Burry Point, Wales in the monoplane *Friendship*, Miss Amelia Earhart, with William Stutz and Lonis Gordon, was the first woman to fly non-stop across the Atlantic.

The same week, Miss Mabel Boll was at Harbour Grace with Captain Oliver Le Boutillier and Arthur Ayles with her plane the *Columbia* awaiting favourable flying conditions, but abandoned her attempt after learning of Earhart's success.

October 17, 1928– Lieutenant Commander MacDonald took off from Harbour Grace in a tiny Moth aircraft on a flight to London on the Alcock and Brown route. After passing a ship 700 miles from Newfoundland, he was never heard from again

October 22, 1929– U.F. Diteman, flying a Barling monoplane named the *Golden Hind*, left Harbour Grace in an attempt to reach London. He was never heard from again.

June 24, 1930– Captain Charles Kingsford Smith, Evan Van Dyke, J. Patrick Saul and J. W. Stannage flew from Port Mannoch, Ireland to Harbour Grace in the *Southern Cross*. They refueled and proceeded on to New York.

October 9, 1930 – The Ballanca monoplane *Columbia*, with Captain Errol Boyd and Lieutenant Harvey Connor, arrived in Newfoundland from Nova Scotia, and later departed from Harbour Grace. They landed in Tresco, Ireland and proceeded to Croydon to complete the first Atlantic crossing from Canada to England.

Around the World Flyers

June 28, 1931– Two famous flyers of the 1930s, Wiley Post and Harold Gatty, left Harbour Grace in their monoplane *Winnie Mae* and arrived in Chester, England 15 hours, 17 minutes later. They broke the record set twelve years before by Alcock and Brown. Two years later Post, flying alone, clipped nearly a full day off the world record they set in 1931, of 8 days, 15 hours, 51 minutes.

June 21, 1931– Danish aviators Holgar Hoirlis and Otto Hillig attempted a flight from Harbour Grace to Copenhagen in the Ballanca monoplane *Liberty*. They came down at Bremen, 240 miles short of their objective.

July 15, 1931– In their monoplane *Justice for Hungary*, Captain George Endres and Alexander Magyar flew from Harbour Grace to Budapest, Hungary.

May 13, 1932 – Lou Reichers, while attempting a solo flight from Newark, New Jersey to Paris, France, took off from Harbour Grace in his Lockheed plane *Liberty* and was rescued from sea by the liner *President Roosevelt*. He was fifty miles from Ireland.

First Solo Woman

May 20, 1932 – The first solo flight across the Atlantic by a woman was made by Amelia Earhart Putnam, who flew from Harbour Grace to Londonderry, a distance of 2000 miles, in 14 hours, 21 minutes.

The DO – X

May 21, 1932 – The largest airliner of her day, the German monoplane DO-X, after flying from New York to Holyrood, via Dildo, NL, took off and proceeded to Vigo, Spain by way of the Azores.

July 5, 1932 – In an attempt to lower the world record of Post and Gatty, set in 1931, the globe flyers, James Mattern and Captain Bennett Griffin flew from New York to Harbour Grace and left again for Berlin. They were forced down, uninjured, near Minsk, Russia.

August 23, 1932 – The Norwegian airmen Thor Solberg and Carl Peterson, in the plane *Enna Jettick*, made a forced landing in Paradise Sound, Placentia Bay, while en route to Oslo from New York via Harbour Grace. Their plane was demolished in the incident.

August 24, 1932 – Clyde Lee and John Brockton, flying in the *Green Mountain Boy* from Vermont on a Trans-Atlantic flight, made a forced landing at Burgeo, NL. They resumed their flight after some minor repairs and went on to Harbour Grace. From there they went on to Oslo, Norway and completed the 3,200-mile journey in thirty-four hours.

August 30, 1932 – Colonel Hutchinson and his Flying Family, in their ten–passenger, twin-motored Sikorsky amphibian, landed at Hopedale, Labrador, en-route to Europe from Port Menier. The plane was wrecked at Greenland and the Flying Family rescued by the steamer *Lord Talbot*.

The Italian Armada

July 12, 1933 – The *Italian Armada* commanded by General Balbo arrived at Cartwright, Labrador en–route to the Chicago World Fair from Rome. They set down at Shoal Harbour, Newfoundland on July 28, 1933 on their return trip to Rome and departed again on August 8. It was the largest mass formation flight of aircraft up to that date.

July 12, 1933 – Mr. and Mrs. Charles Lindbergh arrived at Bay Bulls Big Pond while on a survey flight of the air route from New York to Greenland. Initially, Lindburgh had trouble finding Bay Bulls and set down on Quidi Vidi Lake to seek directions.

August 9, 1933 – The two Polish flyers, Benjamin and Joseph Adamowitz, bound for Warsaw, Poland from New York, crash-landed at the Harbour Grace airfield.

To Baghdad

August 8, 1934 – Captain Leonard Reid, son of Sir William Reid, and a former resident of Newfoundland, and Captain James Ayling left Canada on a flight to Baghdad in an effort to lower the long distance air record but were forced down at Essex, England. The plane was called the *Trail of the Caribou*.

October 29, 1936 – Captain J.A. Mollison in his Ballanca monoplane *Dorothy* flew from Harbour Grace to Groydon, England in 13 hours 17 minutes.

Survey Flights

July 5. 1937 – Pan American *Clipper III* took off from Botwood, NL for Foynes, Ireland on a survey flight for Trans–Atlantic Air Service, making the trip in 12 hours, 34 minutes. On the return journey, it reached Botwood on July 16 and proceeded on to Port Washington after a brief stop.

Simultaneously, the Imperial Airways *Caledonia* flew from east to west and reached Botwood, NL in 16 hours, 24 minutes, later proceeding on to Port Washington, New York. On the return trip across the Atlantic, she left Botwood on July 15 and completed the trip in 12 hours 16 minutes.

August 1937 – Two more trans-Atlantic survey flights were made by way of Botwood by Imperial Airways flying boats, *Caledonia* and *Cambria*. The former set a new record from Botwood to Foynes of 11 hours 33 minutes and the latter a record in the opposite direction of 14 hours, 24 minutes.

July 1938 – The upper component of Imperial Airways four-engine piggy-back plane *Mercury* flew nonstop from Foynes, France to Montreal, Canada, a distance of 3,240 miles, in 22 _ hours, later proceeding to New York with the first commercial load on a North Atlantic flight by a heavier than air craft.[3] On the return trip *Mercury* refueled at Botwood, NL.

Aviation Marvel Starts from Newfoundland

The following item appeared in the *Newfoundlander* on November 7, 1940:

The world was electrified last month when it learned that an airplane had taken off from Harmon Field,

---

3. "Heavier than air craft," in the 1930s referred to airplanes.

Stephenville and crossed the Atlantic to England without having any of its controls touched by human hands, after which it returned to Harmon Field, in the same manner. This latest advance in the world of aviation is called the automatic plane and carries an automatic pilot with an automatic "brain." Although there were eleven people, army officials, scientists, etc., on the return trip to Harmon Field, none of them had any work to do as far as the piloting, etc., was concerned, and were actually only passengers on the automatic aircraft.

Chapter 6

On Land Adventure

Top Secret Mission – Get Rommel

A young soldier from St. John's, Newfoundland, played a key role in one of World War II's most intriguing and adventurous top-secret operations. The objective of the mission was to capture Hitler's top general and military strategist, with hopes that it would boost the morale of the allied forces, and perhaps change the course of the war. The Newfoundlander was Joe Kearney, a resident of 11 Livingstone Street in St. John's.

During the autumn of 1941, twenty-year-old Joseph Kearney was serving with the 57th Newfoundland Regiment at Norfolk, England. Like many in his regiment, Joe was thirsting for adventure on the battlefront. It wasn't surprising that when volunteers were sought to train for a top-secret mission, Joe was one of those to step forward to accept the challenge. There were actually twenty Newfoundlanders who volunteered for the mission, but not all survived the training. Colonel G.W.L. Nicholson, C.D. commented on the fact that so many Newfoundlanders were willing to participate in a highly dangerous mission. Nicholson felt their enthusiasm was inspired by a sense of patriotism, "...instilled in them by their fathers, and also because they were afraid the war would end before they could see action." [1]

The volunteers were assigned to the 11th Scottish Commandos, and given special training in desert survival and combat. The final selection of the men who would participate in the mission was made following a rigorous period of training at Ayrshire, Scotland. The 'Commando' training, no doubt, cured the humdrum existence the Newfoundlanders complained of during their artillery training in England.

Commando training was rough, and only the strongest and most durable survived. A period of rugged intensified training followed to prepare for a treacherous coastal landing in Africa, and survival in a foreign, sometimes hostile environment. Only five of the twenty Newfoundlanders who had volunteered for the mission were selected. The five included: Joe Kearney, Aiden Abbott, Bert

1 Nicholson, Colonel G. W. L., *More Fighting Newfoundlanders*, published by the Newfoundland Government 1969.

'Trapper' Holden, Noel Wood and Jack Reynolds. Kearney was promoted to the rank of Corporal. The training program for those selected became even more severe. It included forced twenty-mile marches that sometimes went even greater distances. Each march would be followed the next day with a man being put overboard at sea in full kit with orders to swim ashore and rendezvous at a pre-determined location by dawn the following day.

The commandos' secret mission was temporarily interrupted when the Germans launched an invasion at Crete. The 11th Scottish Commandos, from which the mission took its volunteers, were issued orders to depart for the Middle East in January 1941. These volunteers had still not been informed of the objective of the mission they had been trained to undertake. They first had to defend Cyprus against an expected German invasion. The anticipated invasion did not happen, and the unit was reassigned to Syria. The Vichy-French, who were allies of the Germans, were strong in this region.

When the 11th Scottish landed on the beaches between Tyre and Sidon, they suffered heavy casualties. They were quickly pinned down by the French, and in the battle that followed seventy percent of the 11th Scots were put out of action, including all the officers. Stranded on the beaches, the commandos were caught between French fire and the Royal Navy's bombarding of the beaches.

According to Nicholson, "Miraculously the five Newfoundlanders escaped injury." The battle ended the 11th Scottish as a fighting unit, and the Newfoundlanders were split up. Although there are gaps in available records regarding the mission to get Hitler's General Rommel, the story picks up with the commandos selected for the mission to capture the general, known as the 'Desert Fox', being divided into two units with each unit being assigned to a submarine. The two submarines were the *Talisman* and the *Torbay*. Not surprisingly, Kearney, the Newfoundlander in the unit, was assigned to the *Torbay*.

The plan slowly unfolded without a hitch. The *Talisman* and *Torbay* successfully landed the commandos on the African coast, and the subs remained in the area to pick the men up after their mission had ended. It was late in November 1941 when the commandos penetrated German lines, and successfully won access to Rommel's headquarters. However, the unit failed to achieve its objective because Rommel was someplace else that evening. The Germans put up a strong resistance which slowed the escape of Kearney's unit.

Kearney, a Tommy-gunner at the time, fought side by side with the commandos' leader, Colonel Geoffrey Keyes, who was killed during the attack. Keyes was posthumously awarded the Victoria Cross.

The Commandos escape plan was foiled by bad weather. Kearney's unit was unable to make it to the coast for a rendezvous with the *Torbay* and attempted to evade capture by making their way inland. For eight days they battled the elements through desert and hills without food or warm clothing to protect themselves from the freezing temperature of desert nights. A joint Italian-German patrol, sent out by Rommel, caught up with them, and all eight were taken prisoner.

The *Evening Telegram* reported in 1959 that Kearney's experience in the German prison camp was a nightmare. The routine of life in a POW camp involved discipline, solitary confinement, punishments, forced labor, starvation diets, bitter cold, illness, and a feeling of futility, which Kearny endured for four years. Recalling this nightmare, Kearney told the *Evening Telegram*:

Christmas Day was just like any other horrible prison camp day. Just twenty-four hours to be lived out, as long as the spirit and the flesh were able to hold out. Christmas dinner, if we were lucky and Red Cross parcels were available, we could live, comparatively, like kings. For example, four men shared one parcel containing perhaps a small tin of fish paste, a tin of meat paste, one bar of chocolate, a quarter pound of butter, sometimes five cigarettes. Most of the time, however, there were no smokes. The contents of the parcel would augment the normal meal of potato soup and black bread. If the Red Cross parcel was not there for

Christmas dinner, we had just soup. Oh yes! There would be a little package of tea or coffee.

It's funny, but my most vivid memory of any of the four Christmases spent as a prisoner-of-war, is of 1943, at a German-run prison camp in Austria. One of the prisoners had received a record player through the Red Cross, and I heard for the first time, Bing Crosby sing White Christmas. *I'll never forget it.*

After returning home from the war, Kearney married and had two daughters, Donna and Joanna.

Newfoundland's Best

A letter written by a Newfoundland soldier, less than a week after the famous Battle of Beaumont Hamel, presented one of the most moving first-hand accounts of the heroism of Newfoundlanders on July 1, 1916. The letter, written by Bert Ellis to his mother Mrs. J. E. Ellis, 60 Springdale Street, St. John's, Newfoundland, was published in the *Evening Telegram* on July 22, 1916 under the heading "The Story of Their Heroism - A sight never to be forgotten."

My Dear Mother,

How glad I am to be able to write to you once again even though I have to do it on my back. I have a lot to be thankful for. No doubt you have heard all about our big drive by this time, or you will by the time you get this. I will try and tell you as briefly as possible how it happened. The Newfoundland Regiment in France is about done. They stood to their guns almost to the last man, and fought like those who knew no fear. When the roll was called only (43) forty-three answered it, and out of that number (2) two were from C Company. Certainly that's not counting the wounded, but I can't say how many were killed or wounded. I think there were more wounded than killed.

We got out of our trenches on Saturday (July 1st) morning, about 9:30. It was a lovely morning, and one never to be forgotten by British soldiers. The 29th Division had one of the worst parts of the line to take, and they took it, but what a price they paid, what a sacrifice of our bravest and our best. It unnerves me to think of it. In the Division are three brigades, the 86th, 87th, and 88th. The last one was attached to altogether between 16,000 and 20,000 men. The 86th had to take the first line, the 87th the second, and we had to take the third line of trenches. Well, our men fell so fast that we had to go up and reinforce the 86th Brig. The first Brig had nothing to compare with like what we had.

It was like Hell let loose. The smoke of guns and noise of shells bursting was something never to be forgotten, not to speak of the machine gun fire, which mowed our men down like wheat before the scythe. No doubt you know what a noise the 'air hammer' makes at the dock when they are working; well, that's something like a machine gun sounds when in action. They played havoc with our men, and to make matters worse, they had practically on both sides, what is called enfilading fire, which is the worst kind of fire to be under. You could almost see the bullets coming; they came so thick and fast. I got over between the first and second lines before I got hit. I got it in the right leg about 4 inches from the ankle, and strange to say, the first one was a bullet, then a piece of shell struck me in the same place.

When I was crawling back, (that's what puzzles me most — however I got back). I was all alone, and never met a soul all the way back (which was about 400 yards) only dead! dead! everywhere!

The awful sight, it made me so sick that I used to lie down, and wonder if I would go on or stay there. It wouldn't have been so bad only they turned the guns on us as we were trying to get back. Our boys acted throughout like heroes. They went up on top singing just as if they were going on a march, instead of facing death. The place we went over, or just in front of us was called the 'Happy Valley' or 'The Vale of Death.'

It put me in mind of Buckmaster's Field, with the German trenches on LeMarchant Road, and ours up by 'Adams,' so when we came on the sky line they just mowed us down, but our boys showed no fear.[2] It will be some time before I can walk, but my leg is not broken for which I can thank God. Tom Kelly's brother Ern is in the same ward with me, so you can tell Tom he is wounded, in the right arm, so it will be a bit difficult for him to write for some time.

The shrapnel bullet went right through his arm, just above his wrist. Tell the family the same address as mine will do for him, and will find him all right. Well, dear, I think this must do for the present as I find it a bit tiresome on my back. Everything possible is done for us here, so don't worry about me. Cheer up, and don't be downhearted. Love to all the friends at home, we will have victory soon.

Yours with love,
B Bert.

City of St. John's Archives
The Newfoundland Regiment were camped in tents at Quidi Vidi before going overseas.

2. Buckmaster's Field is now Buckmasters Circle. Adams, refers to the family residence of former Mayor William Adams at the corner of Adams Avenue and Pennywell Road.

A strategic plan devised to protect soldiers during battle back-fired, and instead, contributed to the casualties during the July 1st Drive. Each soldier had been required to sew on a triangular piece of tin 18 cm. (7 in.) on each side on the back of his uniform between the shoulders to identify allied soldiers for the aircraft providing air cover during battle. However, the sun reflecting off the metal pinpointed wounded soldiers attempting to return to their lines, and made them easy targets for enemy snipers.[3]

The men going into the Battle of the Somme carried with them the following equipment: a rifle with 170 rounds of small-arms ammunition, one iron ration, rations for the day of the assault, two sandbags in belt, two mill grenades, steel helmet, smoke helmet in satchel, water bottle and a haversack on back, field dressing and identity discs. The weight of the above items was sixty pounds. In addition, some men were selected to carry picks, shovels, flares, wooden pickets, mauls, sledge hammers, wire cutters, hedging gloves, a haversack for carrying Lewis gun magazines, bangalore torpedo and trench bridges.

At roll call on July 2, of the 768 Newfoundlanders who fought in the battle, only sixty-eight were present for roll call. By the end of the Battle of the Somme, the total losses for British Forces were 19,240 dead and 38,230 wounded.

Sailor Armed With Axe Gets Victoria Cross

During WWI George Henry Rideout of Pilley's Island, Notre Dame Bay, penetrated enemy lines, knocked out a German communications centre, and killed and wounded several German soldiers with no other weapon but an axe.

Rideout's outstanding display of courage occurred during August 1917 on a battlefield in Serbia near the town of Ansoner. Three thousand British forces were pinned down by German-Austrian forces in an almost continuous barrage of gunfire. The enemy and British forces were entrenched almost two miles apart.

---

3. Smallwood, Joseph R., Editor-in-Chief, *Encyclopedia of Newfoundland and Labrador*, Newfoundland Publishers (1967) Limited.

The open ground between them was filled with shell-torn pits and craters from the ongoing battle.

Rideout, a member of the Royal Navy Reserve, was one of 3000 British soldiers pinned down near Ansoner. On the day of Rideout's heroic act, the Germans had maintained an endless bombardment of British trenches, and men were dying by the hundreds.

In order to understand the situation the British found themselves in that day, it is necessary to describe the battlefield positioning of the troops. On the left flank of the Germans, which was to the right of the battlefield, and slightly towards the front was an enemy observation point. The Germans stationed in this position were able to determine the British range, and telephone the information to their gunners. This information enabled the Germans to drop shells directly in and around British trenches.

Unless something was done to knock out the 'Observation Post,' the British forces faced being wiped out. The British quickly gathered intelligence showing that the wires of the telephone at the Observation Post ran from a tower through a communications trench, to the German batteries, and the British distance from these batteries was easily measured and acted upon.

Between 12:00 and 12:30 that night, the intensity of enemy fire had increased, and British soldiers were falling all around. It was at this point that Rideout and two others volunteered to go forward over the parapet, cross the shell-torn ground, right up to the communication centre where they would cut the wires to put German communications out of commission.

In describing Rideout's mission a year later, the *Evening Telegram* reported, "To think of this was not the noble part. It was the voluntary offering to carry it out that was noble." The British Command agreed to the plan, and Rideout set out with his two companions on their daring mission, with nothing but an axe each for a weapon.

The Germans had anticipated the enemy would try to destroy their communication operation, and to protect it, had stationed snipers at intervals along the telephone lines. The three volunteers slipped quietly over the top and into no-man's-land. Slowly they made their way towards the German lines. The battle continued to rage. Machine gun and rifle fire were so fierce, relentless and deadly that the trio had to drop flat on their stomachs into the first available shell hole.

The short, consistent flashes of light, caused by exploding shells and bombs, provided sufficient brightness for the trio to keep moving towards their target. Their advance was made in short leaps and bounds from one shell hole to another, constantly dodging bullets and the scanning eyes of the snipers.

Just before reaching their target, a bullet struck one of the volunteers and killed him instantly. The remaining two were not deterred. They bravely moved forward until they found themselves in a pit just in time to avoid detection by a passing German sentry. The gunfire was so incessant, and the risk of being caught so great, that they were forced to remain motionless in the pit for one hour.

Suddenly, an opportunity presented itself to complete their mission. A short interruption in gunfire enabled Rideout to make it over the remaining few yards to the German communication lines, and with a few well placed slashes with his axe, he severed the wires and silenced the batteries.

By this time, a German sentry had seen Rideout's shadow moving over a clay background. The sentry rushed towards Rideout with rifle and fixed bayonet, and challenged him. On July 18, 1919 the *Evening Telegram* described the fight that ensued:

> *With a side jump, Rideout avoids him — with an upward, and side slash of his axe, the German is stretched to the ground — dead. But the noise has brought another German, and then another. Again, the axe is brought into play — again a German pays the penalty.*

When Rideout was later asked how many of the enemy he had killed, he answered, "I didn't have time to count." Getting back to the British trenches was just as treacherous as the advance to the German line. A bullet, accidentally directed from the British side, struck and killed Rideout's partner.

City of St. John's Archives
Throughout WWII there was a strong military presence in St. John's.
This photo shows American troops and tanks parading up Military Road.

City of St. John's Archives
This machine gunner was stationed at an artillery battery at the Hill O'
Chips in St. John's during WWII.

Near the home-trenches, a British sentry challenged Rideout, who responded, "Britisher, I'm Rideout." The Newfoundlander was quickly surrounded and cheered by his fellow soldiers. The six-hour mission had ended in success, and although two of the three volunteers had lost their lives, hundreds of lives were saved by their bravery.

For his bravery, Rideout was awarded the Victoria Cross.[4] He was described as 'Newfoundland's Ace' because of the awards he had earned. These included the Egyptian Star, which was presented by the Khedive of Egypt for service as a gunner on H.M.S. *Arphis* in shelling and capturing the towns of Gaza, Jaffa, and Beirut. Rear Admiral G. Jackson added a bar to this medal, the Royal Serbian Silver Medal that was presented to him at Belgrade by the Crown Prince of Serbia. He was also awarded the British Star and the Romanian Medal of Bravery.

The Gallant Jack Legrow of Bauline

When a flotilla of the Royal Navy launched an attack on the 'German-Axis' held Madagascar, Leading Seaman Jack Legrow was not part of the landing crew. However, his courage and quick thinking brought him into the middle of the battle where he successfully assisted fellow seaman who had been pinned down on a beach by an unrelenting enemy assault.

Legrow was a resident of Bauline, a small community just north of St. John's, and a crewman on one of the 11th (*Empire Pride*) Landing Craft Flotilla. On September 10, 1942, the flotilla moved into formation for an attack at Green Beach, at Majunga, on the west side of the 900-mile-long island of Madagascar.

The flotilla launched its attack from a position about 1/4 mile from Green Beach. At about 250 yards from the beach the flotilla was subjected to a vigorous attack from enemy machine gun fire. All the boats brought up bows onto the sea wall. The Army Officer in Legrow's boat, along with two gunners, scrambled up on to the wall and began firing at a house overlooking the beach where enemy fire was originating.

The remaining troops were pinned down by the machine gun fire and were unable to follow the others onto the sea wall. Leading Seaman Jack LeGrow quickly assessed the danger to his fellow sol-

4. *Evening Telegram*, July 18, 1919, pg 9.

diers and moved into action. He reduced speed to 'slow ahead' and moved to a position where he was able to set up his climbing ladder against the wall. With bullets whizzing all around him, LeGrow climbed onto the wall, steadied the ladder and helped pull the troops up. As each man made it to the top, he dropped in position and returned enemy fire. During this entire action the enemy machine gun fire was focused on LeGrow's boat. Although completely exposed, LeGrow continued his effort, showing no concern for his own safety. The attack on the beach was a success and the commanding officer of the flotilla documented LeGrow's act of heroism. The coolness and gallantry displayed by Jack LeGrow under enemy fire earned him the Distinguised Services Medal.

Tommy Ricketts

Thomas Ricketts enlisted in the Newfoundland Regiment on September 2, 1916. The same Thomas Ricketts who lied about his age to get into the Regiment at the height of World War I was on January 19, 1919, at Sandringham Palace to receive the Victoria Cross for courage and heroism from His Majesty the King of England.

The event attracted many members of Royalty including Prince Olaf of Norway, Queen Mary, Queen Alexandria, Queen Maud of Norway and Princess Victoria. There was a great deal of interest in the investiture of Ricketts with the V.C. because of his age. 'Tommy' Ricketts as his friends knew him was just eighteen years old and became the youngest person ever to receive the award. The oldest person awarded the Victoria Cross at the time was sixty-three year old Sir Dighton Probyn, who was among the guests at the palace to congratulate the young Newfoundlander.

Tommy Ricketts' amazing act of heroism took place during the battle of Courtrai in Belgium on October 14, 1918 near Ledgeham. Three divisions of the German-Axis troops were advancing in an attempt to capture part of a railroad which held great strategic importance. The first battallion of the Royal Newfoundland Regiment was advancing with the 9th Regiment.

Allied forces moved forward over a ridge through barbed wire entanglements, crossed a field sown with beet and were stopped at a shallow ditch by a heavy barrage of German gunfire. German soldiers were barricaded inside two nearby farm houses with field guns and machine guns. The ditch afforded little protection for the allied forces, and the Germans shot down many of them.

The troops could neither advance nor retreat, because the enemy had a complete sweep of the field with their artillery. Ricketts volunteered to go forward with Lance Corporal Matthew Brazil of "B" Company, at great personal risk, to try and capture the enemy battery. They moved forward in short bursts to the extreme right of the enemy, in an attempt to outflank them. The two soldiers succeeded in getting to about three hundred yards where they ran out of ammunition. When the Germans realized that an effort was

Photo Submitted
Tommy Ricketts, recipient of the Victoria Cross.

being made to clear their attacking wave, they took steps to move their guns back to a safer position. Ricketts anticipated the German move, and he took it upon himself to go back through the hail of gun fire to get more ammunition. After collecting the ammunition, he dodged bullets all the way back to where he had left Brazil protecting the Lewis Gun.

The young Newfoundlander loaded the gun, and then went on the offensive against the German position. He used the gun so effectively that the Germans retreated and took refuge in an abandoned farm where they were subsequently captured. This brave act of Ricketts enabled the platoon, under Lieutenant Stan Newman, to move in on the Germans without suffering any casualties. They took eight German prisoners, four field guns, and four machine guns. When a fifth enemy field gun started to fire on them, they easily captured that as well. By sunset that day, the Royal

Newfoundland Regiment had taken 500 prisoners and 94 machine guns, eight field guns, and large quantities of ammunition. This accomplishment was not made without great sacrifice. At dawn next day, the Battalion could muster only 300 rifles.

Newfoundland's young hero had a private conversation with His Majesty the King during the presentation of the Victoria Cross at Sandringham Palace. The King asked Ricketts if he remembered the visit of the *HMS Ophir* to Newfoundland at the beginning of the century. Ricketts answered that he did not. His Majesty then related several anecdotes about his reception in Newfoundland. In particular, his recollection of a handsome set of antlers he had viewed in the window of a Water Street store. "I was greatly taken with that head," said the King. "I have often tried to remember the address of the place where I saw it, as I was always anxious to secure it."

The King and Queen, along with their daughter Princess Victoria, took Ricketts on a tour through the grounds of Sandringham. Not only was Thomas Ricketts honored by Britain, he was also recognized by the Government of France, which awarded him the French Croix de Guerre.[5]

Part of his citation reads, "By his presence of mind in anticipating the enemy's intention and his utter disregard of personal safety, Ricketts secured a further supply of ammunition which directly resulted in these important captures and undoubtedly saved many lives."

When Tommy Ricketts returned home to Newfoundland he was given one of the greatest welcomes ever given a Newfoundland hero. The Great War Veterans Association of Newfoundland through public subscription set up an annuity fund for him. Ricketts used his annuity to become a pharmacist. When the King presented Ricketts with the Victoria Cross, he noted that out of seven million soldiers only five hundred had earned the distinction of being awarded the Victoria Cross.

Tommy Ricketts used his annuity fund to become a pharmacist. In the early 1960s well known pharmacist Brian Healy apprenticed

5. *The Newfoundland Magazine*, April 1919 by Captain L. C. Murphy a witness to Rickett's heroism.

with the famous Victoria Cross winner at Ricketts Drug Store on the corner of Job Street and Water Street in St. John's.

Labrador – Scout Hero

Being a Boy Scout in Labrador during the 1940s required courage, endurance and dedication. The Scouts took on responsibilities for services in the North that would be unimaginable by Boy Scout troops elsewhere. During the winter of 1941 several residents of the North owed their survival to the Boy Scouts of Labrador. In one case a very sick woman's survival depended on the Boy Scouts walking fifty miles to the Mission Station to get help. In another situation a man and his child, lying helplessly ill in their one room shack, depended on the arrival of a Boy Scout who stayed for several days, and cared for the two day and night, until they recovered. Unfortunately, the names of these boys were not mentioned in the following report, but considering the nature of the Labrador Boy Scout Movement, there must have been volumes of such reports.

During the 1940s there was a Boy Scout Troop operating at Kakkovik, Northern Labrador. In August 1941 Scoutmaster of the group, A. Perrault, recorded two acts of heroism by members of his troop. The Scoutmaster's report read: "During the past winter there were several cases of sickness and several of the boys had to leave their work and hurry to the Mission Station for medicine and help." The following cases in particular are worth recording.

One of the Scouts had been in the country trapping, and for eleven days he had been walking on snowshoes. He arrived at a log cabin at the head of one of the bays, about sixty miles from the Mission Station, and found a young woman there who was very sick. He was very tired, but after a cup of tea and a bite to eat, he hurried on to his own home, a distance of thirty miles. There he had about two hours rest, and started off again to walk another eight miles over hills. He then reached a log cabin where another member of the scouts lived. He passed on the message and within a very short time this other member was speeding on his way on snowshoes to the Mission Station, a distance of another twelve miles.

The weather was most disagreeable and it was a hard walk against blinding snow and wind, but after about four hours, the message was delivered, and one hour afterward a team of dogs and a komatic with two men took medicine and help to the sick woman.

According to the same report another Scout stayed at a log cabin where he had carried medicine for miles to a very sick child and a man, and looked after them for several days until they recovered.

RCAF World War II Bombs Dumped Outside Harbour

During March 1946, the RCAF in Newfoundland sent sixty tons of bombs left over from the War to be dumped in waters off the coast of St. John's. The handling of the bombs while being loaded on the RCAF motor vessel *Beaver* caused some concern in the city. The job of moving 500 pound bombs was assigned to longshoremen on the waterfront. In describing the scene at the coastal wharf, the *Evening Telegram* noted, "Longshoremen were pushing around 500 pound bombs like sacks of oats or any other supposedly safe commodity as they loaded them aboard the boat from railway freight cars."

The plan to get rid of the bombs was drawn up by the Canadian Navy and involved taking the shipment out to sea and dumping it into the ocean at a spot designated by the Navy. Authorities assured the public the bombs were no longer dangerous. A Navy spokesman said, "The detonators were removed at Gander, placed in a pile and exploded."

Once the bombs were loaded, an experienced bomb disposal group from the Navy took over the cargo and the job of getting rid of it.

This was not the only shipment of unused war bombs sent out to sea from St. John's Harbour. Several months before, the S.S. *Meigle*[6] destroyed a similar cargo.

Threat to St. John's from Unexpected Source

While authorities were concerned over the German attacks upon Bell Island and the sinking of the *Caribou*,[7] a threat to the city of St. John's which was constant throughout the war, and which came close to wiping out a portion of the city on several occasions, went unnoticed. This threat was not from the enemy, but from American bombs arriving at the Army Dock in the east of end of St. John's, and transported to be stored in Quanset Huts at the White Hills, then part of the US base, Fort Pepperrell.

On several known occasions, only good fortune avoided major explosions in the east end of St. John's. During the first such occasion in 1943, it took six trailer-loads of bombs to unload the American munitions ship in port. A driver for one of the trailers, Mike Cahill, recalled that the bombs were loaded during a heavy rain storm. After the loading was completed, and just before the drivers were to get into the trailer cabs to drive off in convoy form, the rain storm escalated into a thunder and lightning storm.

A flash of lightning which Cahill said, "Came out of nowhere," struck one of the bombs. Immediately, the bomb heated up and everyone scattered for cover. "There were a lot of silent prayers that night," said Cahill.

One of the other drivers figured that if he could get a wet tarpaulin over the bombs it would cool them down and avoid an explosion. If even one of the bombs had exploded, it would have set off the hundreds of bombs close by.

---

6. The *S.S. Meigle* was used as a prison ship in St. John's Harbour during the 1930s when overcrowding occurred at the Penitentiary on Forest Road. During WWII the ship had been reconditioned and put into the cargo trade between Newfoundland and Canada. The *Meigle* ended its career during July, 1947 at the 'Graveyard of the Atlantic,' St. Shott's, Ferryland District. It ran ashore when bound for St. John's with a cargo of livestock and General Cargo from Prince Edward Island.

7. The *Caribou* was sunk off Port aux Basques by a German submarine in 1942. The story of the *Caribou* is told in *Newfoundland Disasters* by Jack Fitzgerald, released in 2005 by Creative Publishers.

The tarpaulin caught fire from the heat generating from the bombs. Then it seemed that prayers were answered. The fire burned out as quickly as it started, and the pelting rain cooled down the bombs. The workers were able to move out with their cargoes and deliver them without incident to the White Hills.

On another occasion, flares and bombs were loaded together onto one trailer. The friction caused in loading the cargo set off the flares. Cahill said, "Boy oh boy! What a sight." The flares fired off in all directions. People ran for cover, some ran up the Monkey's Puzzle. (A row of houses that ran up from near the dock to the Battery Road.) The Americans wasted no time in sending in an emergency team to take control of the situation." They succeeded, and another war-time catastrophe was prevented. Either one of the incidents described above could have caused untold destruction of property and loss of life in St. John's. But these were not the only near-miss situations.

Joe O' Toole was driving a load of bombs up over Prescott Street from Water Street when the back hatch, which contained the cargo, broke open. The bombs began falling out and rolling down Prescott Street. Joe quickly turned the vehicle toward the sidewalk, which brought the truck to a parallel position with Duckworth Street, and stopped the bulk of his cargo from emptying onto the street. There was nothing anyone could do about the few that had fallen out except pray. Once again, however, fortune smiled on St. John's and the matter ended without any of the bombs exploding. These incidents had not been revealed to the public until now.

Similar Threat

On March 18, 1945 a similar accident occurred on Prescott Street, but bombs were not involved. Regardless, there was damage but fortunately loss of life was avoided.

At about 11:00 a.m. on Saturday, March 18, an RCAF truck was heading up Prescott Street with a cargo of spools of cable weighing about one and a half tons each. Just past the Water Street intersection the spools broke loose from the truck and began rolling down the hill. Three of the rolls turned at about half-way on

Prescott Street between Duckworth and Water Streets and crashed into the front of the Marguerite Beauty Shop, breaking a large window, and damaging the building somewhat.

The remaining spool continued on to Water Street, where it struck and considerably damaged a car owned by William McArthur, then continued its course into the front of the building occupied by Charles R. Bell Ltd. A large window was also broken in this building, and some heating fixtures were damaged. The driver and helper on the truck shouted warnings to people walking on the street and they all managed to get out of the way of the rolling spools.

Chapter 7

Amazing and Strange
Sea Stories

Ship of Dynamite Burning in St. John's Harbour

A burning ship in St. John's Harbour on November 14, 1895
carried enough explosives to wipe out the hundreds of men,
women and children nearby and to cause major destruction of
property along the St. John's Waterfront. Only the incredible
courage of a handful of firefighters who, although knowing of the
cargo of explosives on board, willingly risked their own lives to
prevent an even greater disaster.

The burning vessel was the *Aurora*[1], a famous whaler of the
time. She was tied up at the Bowring Co.Wharf on the Southside
of St. John's Harbour. Dozens of ships with hundreds of workers
were either tied up nearby or anchored in the harbour. Not far
from the wharves was the Southside Road residential area with
dozens of families. Most of them were out watching the fire. The
city had several fire stations. They were located at Southside
Road, one in the West End, one in Centre Town and one in the East
End.

Fire alarm boxes were placed on poles strategically throughout
the city. Each was connected to the Fire Hall system. In case of fire
the public used these to call in the alarm.

The steamship *Aurora* was a 356 ton vessel and carried a crew
of sixty men. She participated in the whale hunt in the summer of
1895 and had battled hurricane force winds on her return to St.
John's.

It was in November that the *Aurora*, while docked in St. John's
Harbour, had the potential of being the focal point of a major disaster. About six hundred pounds of dynamite and ten thousand
rounds of ammunition were stored below deck. The families,
workers in the area and spectators who came over from the North
side of the harbour had no knowledge of the treacherous cargo in
the *Aurora*.

This drama on the harbour began when Second Officer Tom
Walsh, standing on deck, noticed a trickle of smoke coming up the
companionway. At first, he was not bothered by this, but in min-

1. The *Aurora* is mentioned in the well-known Newfoundland song *The Old Polina*.

utes the smoke began to billow up the companionway. When he went to investigate, he found the cabin directly below full of smoke and the captain's room on the starboard side was engulfed in flames. Stored not far from these flames were the dynamite and ammunition. Walsh alerted captain and crew, and a man was sent to call the alarm at fire-box 43 on Southside Road. While the crew tried to control the fire with what little resources they had, firemen at the West End Station responded to the alarm. They hitched up their horses to the fire wagons, put on their suits and in just six minutes were at White's Wharf, a couple of hundred feet west of Bowrings, and ready to do battle. This was as close as the firemen could get to Bowrings' Wharf that day.

Just as they were getting hoses ready, the Southside Firemen showed up. There was some confusion at first over what to do, but Captain Dunn of the West End Fire Department took control and the firemen worked as a single unit. The two groups combined eight hundred feet of hose to battle the blaze. This hosing extended from White's Wharf down over Stewart's, Tessier's and Bowrings' wharves. Captain Dunn estimated another thirty or forty feet of hose was needed. Although the Central firemen were expected at any minute, Captain Dunn chose not to take a chance. He sent a man back to the West End Fire Hall near Job Street. In a short time, he was back with a sufficient length of hose. When Captain Dunn moved onto the deck of the *Aurora* to take full control of the fire-fighting effort, he was joined by firemen from Central, West End and the Southside fire stations.

The billowing smoke and flames from the burning vessel were attracting spectators from all around St. John's. Some came by foot while others rowed across the harbour. The firemen knew the *Aurora* was carrying explosives and were aware of the potential for disaster. Regardless, Captain Dunn, accompanied by Sgt. Daniel Mulrooney and Fire Constable Reardon, risked their lives to go below deck and into the cabin where but a single wall separated the fire from the explosives. They remained steadfast in position until the fire was out and the threat to the public ended.

The next day the *Daily News* commented on the heroic deed, "They were perfectly aware that at any moment a terrible explosion might occur; that the cabin, in fact, might prove their grave, but duty called and a true fireman knows no fear in such a case."

In a letter to the *Daily News,* an eye witness asked, "What would have been the result had that quantity of powder exploded? Can anyone measure the possibile destruction of life and property likely to have accrued therefrom?" The

City of St. John's Archives
St. John's Harbour scene around the time of the *Aurora* drama.

writer suggested the men be recognized for their outstanding display of courage in risking their lives to bring the fire under control and to avoid certain disaster in St. John's Harbour.

The men were honoured within days by Sir Edgar Bowring, and two years later awarded medals. Sir Edgar Bowring sent a cheque for $100 to Inspector General J.R. McCowan for the men, "...as a slight recognition of the valuable services rendered by the Fire Brigade in so promptly suppressing the fire which broke out on the *Aurora*." In response to this gift, Inspector General McCowan replied, "I feel proud of being in command of such men who, notwithstanding the knowledge of the extreme danger of the position in which they worked, yet performed their duty fearlessly because it was their duty." The danger was even greater than first thought because there were other vessels in the harbour carrying explosives.

Governor Murray was instrumental in having the men awarded medals in recognition for their heroism in fighting that fire. In 1897, in honour of Queen Victoria's Diamond Jubilee, the awards were presented to the following men: To Inspector General McGowan, District Chief Dunn and Fire Constable John Reardon, the Silver Star; to Sergeant Daniel Mulrooney and Fire Constable James Howard, the Silver Medal for conspicuous gallantry and bravery.

During 1895 Kaiser Wilhelm of Germany, perhaps the world's most powerful man at the time, had sent messages to St. John's and England in an attempt to locate Captain William Fitzgerald, a native of Carbonear, Newfoundland. The Kaiser, of whom historian H. F. Shortis had written, "...had only to stamp his foot and the whole world would stop to listen," was anxious to reward the Newfoundland sea captain for the heroic rescue of twenty-six of the Emperor's subjects from a sinking ship during a raging storm in the North Atlantic.

The sea adventure of Captain Fitzgerald had its beginning on December 21, 1893 when he set sail from St. John's in the topsail schooner *Rose of Torridge* bound for Gibralter. On January 24, 1894, he was nearing latitude 36 degrees North and 20 degrees West in a raging wind storm. While Captain Fitzgerald and crew struggled to keep their vessel on course, they were suddenly thrust into an even more treacherous dilemma. Straight ahead was the German vessel *Cassandra,* flying a distress signal that read, "Ship is sinking. Wish to abandon."

Although Captain Fitzgerald never gave any thought to not responding to the distress call, he was baffled over how to get close enough to the *Cassandra* to rescue the crew without losing his own ship and endangering his own men. Captain Fitzgerald skillfully maneuvered his ship in circling the *Cassandra* six times. When it became apparent time was about to run out he moved into action. He brought the *Rose of Torridge* as close to the distressed vessel as possible and began removing the crew.

During the rescue, a block from the loft of the *Cassandra* fell and struck Captain Fitzgerald. If it had not been for his strong physical condition, he might not have survived the mishap. He got to his feet and continued the rescue effort. Fitzgerald later recalled one of the biggest problems at that time was getting the German captain up and over the side of the *Rose of Torridge*. The Captain weighed over two hundred pounds. All twenty-six members of the *Cassandra*'s crew made it safely to Captain Fitzgerald's ship. It was just in time. The stern of the sinking vessel raised high in the water and it nosedived, completely disappearing beneath the crashing waves.

When the *Rose of Torridge* arrived in Gibraltar, the German survivors were taken to the German Consul and a statement was taken from Captain Fitzgerald. The Consul, after confirming the amazing sea rescue, sent a dispatch to the German Emperor. Meanwhile, Captain Fitzgerald continued his trip, and after discharging his cargo took on a load of salt at Trapani before returning to St. John's, Newfoundland.

Courtesy Bob Rumsey
Grave of Captain William Fitzgerald in the Roman Catholic Cemetery at Carbonear.

Upon his arrival at St. John's, he was approached by R.H. Prowse, German Consul to Newfoundland, with a surprising offer from the German Emperor. Kaiser Wilhelm wished to honour Captain Fitzgerald with a special gift in recognition of his heroic rescue of twenty six of the Kaiser's subjects. Prowse asked Captain Fitzgerald to choose a gift from among a list that included a watch, a sextant, binoculars and a medal. The Captain said he would prefer a watch, and Prowse advised the Kaiser by mail of the Captain's preference.

A year passed and Captain Fitzgerald, not having a reply from the Kaiser, had just about forgotten the offer. Then on February

28,1895, while delivering a cargo of fish to Plymouth, England he received a message from the German Consul there telling him that Kaiser Wilhelm II had sent the gold watch Fitzgerald had chosen to Government House at St. John's. He instructed the captain to contact Governor Sir Terrence O'Brien upon his return to Newfoundland and the Governor would arrange for a presentation of the award.

The *Rose of Torridge* was sold at Plymouth and Captain Fitzgerald and crew returned to St. John's on the steamship *Assyrian* of the Allan Line, arriving there on April 15. A message was awaiting him upon departure from the ship advising him to go to Government House at 6:00 p.m. that same day to receive the award given by the German Emperor. Unfortunately, Captain Fitzgerald had to decline the invitation due to an urgent family matter at Carbonear. He was presented with the award at a later date. Historian H.F. Shortis, who said he had held the watch and had seen it a hundred times, described it as being solid gold. He said, "On the back case was a bust of the Emperor in relief and an inscription detailing the circumstance for which the watch was given, and on the bottom a facsimile of the Emperor's signature."

This was not Fitzgerald's only act of heroism. He also rescued the surviving crew members of the 158 ton *Wolverston*, shipwrecked several years later. Ten men had drowned in that shipwreck before Captain Fitzgerald had arrived at the scene.

This author has learned that the historic watch has remained in the hands of a descendant of Captain William Fitzgerald who is now living in Ontario.

Twice a Hero

The captain and crew of a wrecked ship wondered if they would survive their ordeal while they sought safety at the peak of a 100-foot-high rock at the entrance to a gulch near Trepassey. Strong winds and a rising tide added to the near hopelessness of their situation. While they prayed for divine intervention, unknown to them, John Kennedy from Trepassey had witnessed the shipwreck and gone for help. The date was September 1, 1887. Just twenty-four hours before, Captain Richards of the *Maglona* and his crew had set sail from Little Placentia for Bay Bulls to take on a cargo of salt fish for overseas markets. They ran into problems from the start. Marmaduke Clowe, the ship's Supercargo,[2] cursed the strong headwinds which were significantly slowing the ship's advance.

Near Cape St. Mary's, the *Maglona* ran into a heavy fog. Although Captain Richards altered his course, the ship was moving closer than anticipated to the treacherous rocky shores.

The crew had managed to lower the mainsail by the time someone shouted the warning "Breakers!" However, it was too late. The *Maglona* struck rocks and broke its rudder at the entrance to the gulch. The ship's only lifeboat was washed away by a crushing wave as the captain and crew looked on helplessly.

Captain Richards had observed that with each crushing wave that struck the boat, the stern heaved toward a nearby 100-foot-high island rock. He viewed this as a chance for all on board to escape the ship before the waves took it to the bottom. The captain observed that in order to escape, they had to leave from the starboard side, but the heavy main-boom was swinging back and forth across the quarterdeck. He thought that a blow from it could be fatal. One by one, the crew dodged the swinging boom until all had successfully made the move from the *Maglona* to the rock. The joy over successfully abandoning the vessel was short lived when the men found themselves isolated on a rock that was impossible to scale, and cut off from the shore by a treacherous sea and the gulch.

Just as despair was setting in, they heard muffled voices from shore and felt their prayers were answered. Little did they know, their shouts of "help" were not needed. John Kennedy, the man who had witnessed the shipwreck and gone for help, was now back with one Tom Neil and preparing to put a rescue into action. The two had brought two ropes with them, one, a long heavy rope and, the other a lighter rope. Kennedy tied the light rope around Neil and the other end to the heavy rope which he anchored around a large

2. The Supercargo was the person representing the ship's owner and responsible for the cargo.

rock. Neil then plunged into the raging sea. Tom Neil was no stranger to courage and heroism. Just ten years earlier, he had risked his life by scaling a 300 foot cliff in a storm to recover victims of the wreck of the *George Washington*.

The men watched, amazed at the courage of Neil, as he fought through the tossing waves, waves which often tossed him head over heels causing him to disappear. Just when the stranded men thought he was gone, back he would come to the surface and resume his battle to save them. By the time he reached the rock, he was bruised and bleeding, but not beaten. Neil was determined to get every man safely to shore. After untying the light rope around him, Neil, with the help of the stranded men, managed to pull the heavy rope to them. He then secured the rope and one by one, they made their successful escape to shore. Neil, however, was not yet finished. He volunteered to go with the men over seven miles of open barrens, and fought wind and cold rain all the way to Cape Race.

Newfoundland's Marie Celeste

The strange fate of the brig *Resolven* in Newfoundland coastal waters in 1884 remains a mystery to this day, and was described in the 1920s by Journalist Arthur Ainsworth of London as being in the same class as the *Marie Celeste*. A dark cloud seemed to hang over the *Resolven* and there was speculation it was a cursed ship. From the day in August 1884 when news of the ship's strange experience first broke, to the day it was lost in a shipwreck four years later, bad luck seemed to follow it.

The 143 ton *Resolven* was built in Nova Scotia of soft wood, and carried a crew of six men. Her Captain was E. James and it hailed from Abberystwith. The *Resolven* arrived at Harbour Grace on July 14, 1884 with a cargo for John Munn & Co. Ltd. and was under charter to proceed to Labrador to take a cargo of fish to the Mediterranean. She departed Harbour Grace on August 27 and carried four passengers who were going to Labrador to work at trimming herring for John Munn & Co. Ltd. The passengers were Doug Taylor and Bernard Coldford of Carbonear, Edward Keefe of Harbour Grace, and Bill Bennett of Bell Island.

Soon after starting the voyage to Labrador, the *Resolven* experienced a tragedy, the cause of which has remained a mystery since that time. By August 29, just two days after departing, word was received in Harbour Grace that the ship had run into trouble on the Atlantic and was in tow to Catalina by the HMS *Mallard*. Shipwreck and tragedy were not unknown to Newfoundlanders but when people heard the story of the *Resolven*, it sent chills up the spine of many Newfoundlanders and attracted international attention.

The vessel had been found deserted at the mouth of Trinity Bay. A rescue party could find no sign of life on board and a search of the area failed to turn up any trace of the crew, passengers, or anything that would give even the slightest hint of what the *Resolven* had encountered.

The mystery was heightened by the discovery that the sails were set, a fire was alight in the galley and no wreckage or disorder was to be seen. The only thing out of place was the yardarm, which was broken, and some ropes left dangling.

One discovery that gave them hope was that the lifeboat was missing. From all appearances, the crew and passengers had left in a hurry to escape some kind of imminent danger. Not a trace of the men or the missing lifeboat was ever found.

The Raisin Ship

The Raisin Ship was known throughout Newfoundland for decades and nostalgically recalled because of its connection to Newfoundlanders' penchant for figgy-duff pudding. The *Caroline Brown*, which became famous in Newfoundland as the Raisin Ship, was a United States based vessel carrying a cargo of raisins in bulk from Greece to the United States. In Atlantic waters near Newfoundland, it became encircled by a raging winter storm and was abandoned by its captain and crew. Fortunately, they were rescued the next day, having drifted a long distance south of their abandoned ship.

The *Caroline Brown* survived the storm and was found by Captain John Kennedy of Carbonear who took the prize in tow to

Carter-Fitzgerald Photography
Author Jack Fitzgerald researching at Colonial Building Archives.

St. John's. Word rapidly spread throughout the capital city of the enormous cargo of raisins on the rescued ship tied up in the harbour. Small kids went away with their pockets full of raisins, and many more found their way into kitchen ovens as part of a figgy-duff (pudding).

The abundance of raisins in the city prompted the public to refer to the *Caroline Brown* as the Raisin ship and the name stuck. Stories of the Raisin Ship and the figgy-duffs spread to Conception Bay. The vessel was purchased by John Munn & Co. Ltd. and taken to Carbonear with a half cargo of raisins, still aboard. It didn't take long for the women and children of the community to seek out a share of the raisins. Munn's sold them for three cents a pound, but no child was refused a handful of the fruit. Never in Newfoundland's history had so much figgy-duff been eaten by so many people in one season. The abandoning of the Raisin Ship took place in the late 1890s and has been told here to illustrate that our shipwreck history was not always tragic.

The English Refused to Help

Not all shipwrecks bring out the best in people. For example, when the *Blanche*, owned by Job & Co. of St. John's, was abandoned and sunk in the Atlantic, the survivors were not well treated by at least some residents of Dover, England. The adventure of the *Blanche* began on December 7, 1904 when it set sail from St. John's with a cargo of salt cod for Brazil. Captain William Sinclair was in command of the crew of seven men: J. Newhook, mate; J. Caldwell, boatswain; and G. Shave, T, Smith, T. Walsh, J. Glynn and T. Williams, crewmen.

Rarely has a ship encountered as many winter storms on the North Atlantic as the *Blanche* experienced in its terrorizing voyage that year. From the day the *Blanche* sailed out the Narrows of St. John's Harbour, it fought high winds. As the days went by, these winds were replaced by blinding snow storms, blizzards and hurricanes. Captain Sinclair and his crew were experienced seamen who were forced to use all their skills and endurance not only to keep the ship afloat, but to keep themselves alive.

During a blizzard, the foresail burst and the vessel was put under a small reaching canvas. When a hurricane hit, the jibs and headgear were blown away. The hurricane worsened and throughout the night, mountainous waves washed over the *Blanche*. These took with them the mizzen, and the fore gaff topsails were torn to ribbons. While the ship was being dismantled around them, the crew fought against the elements: the winds, gigantic waves and freezing spray, snow pellets like sand cut their skin. A deep hard frost threatened their survival.

Several lulls in the storm allowed the captain and crew some time to attempt repairs. The hurricane hit quicker than anticipated, and they were not prepared for it. None of the crew, including the captain, had ever experienced a storm like it. In the midst of the hurricane the *Blanche* turned over on its side and the men felt the end was near. Nevertheless, they were determined to fight to the best of their ability to the end and they worked throughout the night to cut away the foremast in hopes of righting the ship. By next morning, with the men near exhaustion their efforts and prayers were answered. The ship righted itself.

But their struggle was not yet over. Sometimes they fought the elements waist-deep in water. They cut away the spars and the jibboom until the *Blanche* resembled a floating log. Meanwhile, the lifeboat had washed away in the storm. To keep the vessel afloat, they now had to jettison 300 barrels of their cargo. Another 300 barrels had been lost into the sea when the hold broke open after being smashed by a mountainous wave.

Captain Sinclair told the men their only hope of survival was to make it to the major shipping lane and hope for rescue. On

December 22, at 10:00 a.m., the *Blanche* was spotted by Captain J. Christianson in the SS *Seveland* which was sailing from Sweden to Bremen, Virginia. The Swede sent a lifeboat to rescue the Newfoundlanders.

The courageous Newfoundland crew had survived a three-week battle of the worst of Atlantic storms. The captain knew there was one last duty to perform before abandoning ship. He realized that if he left the ship afloat it would remain as a danger to shipping in the area. He decided to sink the *Blanche* by removing its hatches so it would fill with water and sink. After performing this last duty, Captain Sinclair boarded the lifeboat and was taken with his crew to the safety of the *Seveland.*

Nine days later, the rescue vessel came across a Scottish pilot off Durngeness, but he flatly refused to take the survivors to port. Off the coast of Dover, another pilot vessel was encountered and this time the pilot demanded payment of 1 lb Sterling per man to take the Newfoundlanders to port. This angered the Swedish captain and an angry exchange of words erupted that could have resulted in violence if the English had been closer. Finally, the captain chose to deliver the survivors himself. Despite the captain's efforts, the Board of Trade at Dover refused to take charge of the men as their contracts read that they were to be paid off in Liverpool.

Finally, the Liverpool Shipwrecked Mariners Society took charge of the survivors and on New Year's Day sent them to Liverpool. By mid-January, the captain and crew of the *Blanche* were at home in Newfoundland. They had all experienced a life threatening challenge they had never before dreamed of, nor would they want to again.

Amazing Atlantic Sealers Race

The Newfoundland built *Fanny Bloomer* was one of the most successful sealing ships of the nineteenth century. During that era, she was closely identified with the famous Southern Shore sea-faring family, the Jackmans of Renews. When Captain Thomas Jackman was injured on the *Fanny Bloomer* by a swinging tiller, his son, William, took command. It was his first command and he was a natural. When Bowring Brothers made him a lucrative offer to take command of the *Sally Ann*, he accepted and his brother, Captain Arthur Jackman, took command of the *Fanny Bloomer*. Captain Arthur became one of the most successful sealing captains of Newfoundland history.

The *Fanny Bloomer* and another Newfoundland vessel, the *Mary Belle*, earned notoriety not only as great sealing ships, but for an impromptu race across the North Atlantic during the winter of 1856-1857. This remarkable story began mid-December 1856. The *Fanny Bloomer* was under the command of Captain John Flynn and the *Mary Belle* was under the command of Captain James Day, a former member of the Newfoundland Legislature for St. John's West.

The two ships were being towed down the Mersey in England by the same tug boat, when Captain Day shouted to Captain Flynn, "I'll bet you twenty five pounds I'll be in St. John's before you."

"I can't bet you that much, because I have no money to pay you only out of my wages, but I'll bet ten pounds," answered Captain Flynn.

The race was on. Both crews felt it would add excitement to the long and often treacherous return trip across the Atlantic. Side by side, the *Fanny Bloomer* and *Mary Belle* sailed down Saint George's Channel, England keeping each other in sight for several days. It wasn't smooth sailing and wind and rain storms quickly separated the two rivals. Yet, although out of sight of each other, each Captain never forgot he was in a race. By mid-way, they were again in sight of each other and signals were sent back and forth between the ships. Once again, the oceans tossed and they lost sight of each other until they neared land, at which time they were about three-quarters of a mile apart.

At this point the ships were between Bay Bulls and Petty Harbour. When they caught sight of each other, the competitiveness of the crews showed. On went studding sails and every inch of canvas was hoisted and respective house flags (Bowring's and Tessier's) were posted to the foremast head, as a signal to Cape Spear. The ships passed the Cape as they had started in England, with less than a hundred yards separating them. Finally, after a thirty-eight day crossing, they passed through the Narrows of St. John's Harbour. The Harbour-Pilot boarded Captain Day's vessel first because she was to the windward of the *Fanny Bloomer*. He then boarded the *Fanny Bloomer*. The ships had entered the Narrows the same time and the race was declared a draw. The two ships ended the race as they started, side by side. This was hailed as a remarkable feat and the story became one of Newfoundland's many colourful tales of the sea.

In 1870, Captain Arthur Jackman took a cargo of seal oil and skins to Liverpool in the *Fanny Bloomer*. The ship was sold there and spent the remainder of its years carrying coal between Wales and Waterford Ireland.

Strange Force at Work

Was a supernatural phenomena involved in the rescue of the *Orion* near Bell Island in 1867, or were the strange circumstances leading up to that rescue purely coincidental? Whatever took place it was responsible for saving five men from freezing or starving to death on a shipwrecked vessel.

Captain James Keefe and Captain Nicholas Fitzgerald were best friends. During October 1867, one of them was fighting for survival on the Atlantic and the other was mysteriously drawn towards him by a compelling, but unexplained force. This remarkable tale of the sea started on October 9, 1867, during a heavy wind storm that struck Corbett's Harbour, Labrador. Captain James Keefe of the brigantine *Orion*, his brother and four crew members struggled to put out line to the *Orion* when the near-hurricane-force winds drove the vessel from her moorings.

Before reaching the open sea, the *Orion* struck Coveyduck Island at the harbour's mouth and hung there for a short while. One of the crew managed to jump from the jib-boom and succeeded in reaching dry land. When the others attempted to follow, the badly broken vessel had filled with so much water that only the forward part remained above water. The *Orion* drifted south for four days and, to survive, the men had to tie themselves to the rigging. To obtain food and liquids, one man at a time would unleash himself to get supplies to feed the others. Food was very limited. The only food on the vessel was a supply of dry flour and some fat pork that had been stored in the forecastle; the only dry place left on the *Orion*.

On October 13, with Captain Keefe wondering how much longer he and his crew could survive, his friend, Captain Nicholas Fitzgerald,[3] was departing Snug Harbour, Labrador on a return trip to Harbour Grace. His schooner, the *George H. Fogg*, was considered the fastest vessel in the country. From the start of the trip, Captain Fitzgerald was tormented by something, but had no idea what was bothering him. He felt compelled to change his course and had no explanation to offer his men when he suddenly altered the ship's course by two points. The crew members were puzzled by the change and Fitzgerald had no reason other than he felt compelled to take this action.

Then, about twenty miles east of Bell Island, Captain Fitzgerald spied a wreck and as he approached it, he recognized it as the *Orion* carrying his friend, Captain Keefe. Fitzgerald and his men quickly rescued Keefe and his crew and provided warm blankets, food and refreshments. A day later they were all back at Harbour Grace and celebrated their rescue at Captain Fitzgerald's home.

This amazing story was still being told fifty years after the event, but has long since been forgotten. The mystery as to what force drew Captain Fitzgerald to the *Orion* that day remains unexplained.

Mystery Disappearance of the Southern Cross

While the tragic story of the *Newfoundland* disaster of 1914, with its loss of seventy-eight sealers, was making headlines across Newfoundland, and with public attention focused on that disaster, an even greater tragedy had occurred, but remained unknown for

---

3. This was the same Captain Nicholas Fitzgerald who was given the map to the Lost Treasure of Lima by Captain John Keating. This story is told in *Treasure Island Revisited*, by Jack Fitzgerald, Creative Publishers.

days. The *Southern Cross*, with a crew of 173 men and a bumper cargo of seal pelts, had disappeared, leaving no trace as to what tragic circumstances had overtaken it. Almost one hundred years have passed since its disappearance, and still no evidence has surfaced to shed light on this, the greatest mystery of all Newfoundland marine disasters.

The *Southern Cross*, under the command of Captain John Clarke, sailed from St. John's on March 12, 1914 heading for the annual Gulf seal hunt. Other vessels at the Gulf at the time were the *Terra Nova*, *Neptune*, *Eric*, *Viking* and the *Seal*. It was a practice at the time for ships to telegraph regular progress reports to St. John's where they were posted outside the General Post Office (GPO) on Water Street. After 'tea' each day, crowds would gather outside the GPO to read the latest news on the sealing fleet.

For some unexplained reason, the *Southern Cross* failed to supply any direct progress messages. Instead, other ships relayed progress reports from the *Southern Cross* to St. John's. This suggested that either the vessel had no telegraph machine, or else, if it had one, it had broken down.

On March 30, those with loved ones on the *Southern Cross* were elated by a message which they believed referred to the *Southern Cross*. The message read: "Steamer passing out of the gulf, distant; supposed to be the *Southern Cross* or the *Terra Nova*; flags flying, looked well fished."

Many in the crowd argued that the vessel mentioned in the dispatch was actually the *Terra Nova*. Their optimism was based on previous reports that the *Terra Nova*, just five days before, had 24,000 pelts on board. No reports had been received that mentioned the number of seals taken by the *Southern Cross*.

The attention of the crowd turned to speculating on what date the ship referred to would arrive. By most calculations, it was predicted that if the vessel was the *Terra Nova*, it would arrive in St. John's by Wednesday, April 1, and if it was the *Southern Cross*, she would make Harbour Grace by the same day. The land-based experts added that their predictions were based on the assumption that favorable weather prevailed.

On Tuesday, March 31, nobody suspected that the *Southern Cross* was in trouble. The *Evening Telegram* reported the latest information on the sealer:

> *The* Southern Cross *has not been reported since passing St. Pierre yesterday afternoon, and the general opinion is that she is 'hove to' in Placentia Bay. The night being fine, she evidently passed St. Lawrence and Burin, or she would have been reported from either of these places.*
>
> *Assessing that she reached Dodding Head about 11:00 p.m. yesterday, she would likely shape her course for Cape St. Mary's. As she is heavily laden, and can only steam a little over five knots, she would not be due at Cape St. Mary's until about 8 or 9 o'clock this morning. The storm came on about 7:00 a.m., and experienced mariners venture the opinion that she is about 15 or 20 miles west of Cape St. Mary's.*

The *Newfoundland* disaster occurred on March 31. However, there was still no public alarm over the non-arrival of the *Southern Cross*. On April 1, the *Telegram* reported:

> *Messers. Bowring Brothers Ltd., received a message from Captain Connors of the S. S.* Portia *today, saying that he passed the* Southern Cross *five miles W.N.W. of Cape Pine, at 11:00 a.m. yesterday. It is supposed that she ran into St. Mary's Bay, and harboured at North Harbour.*

Public attention, during this period, was focused on the *Newfoundland* disaster and the loss of seventy eight lives. Consequently, those with loved ones on the *Southern Cross* were becoming anxious. The April 1 message from Captain Connors was the last reference to any sighting of the *Southern Cross*.

On April 3, the Cape Race wireless station reported that the *Southern Cross* had not passed the Cape or Trepassey, and a message from Captain Connors confirmed she had not arrived at St. Mary's Bay. At this point, and while dealing with the tragedy of the

Newfoundland, authorities became alarmed over the fate of the *Southern Cross.* Contact was made by them with the U.S. *Seneca* which was in the vicinity of Cape Race. The *Seneca* was joined by the *Kyle* in a joint search effort for the missing sealing vessel.

Although there was a level of concern over the *Southern Cross,* the public remained optimistic and there was a perception that her delay in returning to St. John's was caused by bad weather. On April 4, the *Evening Telegram* reflected this public optimism, "If she had been driven off to sea, which is the general opinion expressed by experienced seamen, it would take her some days to make land again. The ship is heavily laden, and cannot steam at a great speed."

By April 7, the *Fiona* had joined in the search. Authorities questioned many schooner captains in the area where the *Southern Cross* was last seen, but not a trace of the *Southern Cross* could be found. The only possible clue to the fate of the sealing vessel came on April 11.

The *Kyle* reported seeing two white-coat pelts off Cape St. Mary's while on route to St. John's. The captain explained that due to the weather conditions, visibility was very limited. When the *Kyle* picked up supplies in St. John's, it set out for the Cape St. Mary's area to renew the search for the *Southern Cross.* Days passed into weeks, then months, then decades, and not a trace of the *Southern Cross* was ever found. The ship, its cargo and 173 men disappeared off the face of the earth.

The Edmund B. Alexander Story

The *Edmund B. Alexander,* the American troop ship that brought the first American soldiers to go overseas in World War II to St. John's, Newfoundland, became as much a part of Newfoundland history as any Newfoundland vessel.

Throughout WWII, the sinking of the *Edmund B. Alexander* remained a priority for German U-Boat commanders, with the promise of the immediate conferring of the Iron Cross to the U-Boat commander responsible for destruction of this United States troop carrier. The *Edmund B. Alexander* measured 668 feet in

Courtesy City of St. John's Archives
The *Edmund B. Alexander* docked on the Southside of St. John's Harbour in 1941.

length and was designed to carry 4,000 passengers which was twice the passenger capacity of the *Queen Mary*.

The *Edmund B. Alexander* arrived in St. John's in January 1941, and remained moored on the south side of the Harbour where it was used as a floating barracks for several months while Camp Alexander was being prepared to house troops at Rennies Mill Road and Carpasian Road.[4]

Apart from the historical significance of landing the first American troops in Newfoundland, the *Edmund B. Alexander* had an exciting and adventurous history. The troop carrier was built at an Irish shipyard in 1905 for the German-owned Lloyd Line of passenger ships. It was originally named the *Amerika* to attract passengers from the United States, and operated on the Breman to New York.

One of the first adventures of the *Amerika* involved the *Titanic* disaster. Had the officers of the *Titanic* acted upon warnings and information provided by the *Amerika*, the tragedy could have been avoided. When travelling east-bound on the Atlantic on the afternoon of April 14, 1912, the *Amerika* cautiously encountered and passed through ice fields south of Newfoundland.

---

4. Troops were housed at Camp Alexander until Fort Pepperrel at Pleasantville was completed.

She alerted the *Titanic* and provided the exact locations of the icebergs. It was revealed later at the enquiry into the sinking of the *Titanic* that the *Amerika*'s warning was received and plotted on the *Titanic* charts, but then ignored. The price paid for this mistake is now history.

The *Amerika* had another encounter in 1912 that made news around the world. Unknown to the Captain of the *Amerika,* it was sailing directly in a path that crossed that of the British submarine *S-12.* The captain of the submarine gave orders to surface, and as the craft rose, he took the usual sweep with his periscope. The captain was horrified to see one of the largest ships in the world bearing down on him, just yards away. News reports noted, "He barely had time to shout 'crash dive' before the *Amerika* sliced the submarine in half." Only one person on board the submarine survived the sinking.

In 1914, WWI broke out, and the future of the *Amerika* was changed forever. She was one of ninety German ships caught in neutral and enemy ports, and was interred in New York. The *Amerika* remained there until the United States entered the war in 1917. The 'K' in 'Amerika' was changed to 'C', and as the *America*, she was converted into a troop-transport ship. In her short service in that war, she had carried 40,000 soldiers to France. Once again the *America* was touched with tragedy. While embarking troops at Hoboken, New Jersey, in 1918, she sank with the loss of several lives. Having been re-floated, she was repaired and the vessel was used to carry troops home from Europe at the end of the war.

In 1920, the *America* was assigned to clear up a problem created by the Germans during World War I. In 1915 the Germans conscripted thousands of Czechs into the army, and these troops were sent to the Russian Front. Large numbers of these conscripts were captured by the Russians, and sent to prison camps in Siberia. The *America* sailed from New York in 1920, and traveled through the Panama Canal and across the Pacific Ocean to Vladvistock. In that port, she took the Czechs, who were released from Russian prisons, to the newly created Czech Republic.

In 1929, the *America* was involved in a remarkable rescue at sea. The rescue took place at night during a severe wind storm. The Italian steamer *Florida* was in distress and sinking in the north Atlantic. The *America*'s first officer, Harry Manning, was responsible for the miraculous rescue of the entire *Florida* crew. He is credited with the rescue through a spectacular navigation maneuver which brought the massive vessel close enough to get everyone off the *Florida*. Harry Manning later became Commodore of the United States Lines, and was commanding officer of the luxury liner *United States* on her maiden voyage. In 1932, the *America* was laid up in Maryland, and attempts to sell her were unsuccessful. In 1940, she was fitted out as a troop ship and renamed the *Edmund B. Alexander*, after the man who commanded the 3rd United States Infantry in the Mexican War of 1846-1848. The first assignment of the *Edmund B. Alexander* was to transport American troops to St. John's, Newfoundland. The troop carrier made two trips to the port of St. John's.

The next adventure of the *Edmund B. Alexander* occurred during WWII. In 1942, she had undergone a major overhaul, and converted from coal to oil. While on her last run with troops, she crossed the path of a German U-Boat. The captain, after identifying the ship, saw his opportunity to earn the 'Iron Cross'. The U-Boat had only one torpedo remaining when she sighted the *Edmund B. Alexander*. After shouting "Fire one!", the captain ordered the crew to dive.

An alert lookout on the troop ship saw the submarine's periscope, and the vessel made a successful evasive move, passing over the submarine within inches. The U-Boat moved up to periscope depth in time for the Commander to get a view of the *Edmund B. Alexander* moving off at full speed, and with it, his hopes for the Iron Cross disappearing. At the end of the war, the *Edmund B. Alexander* carried troops home from Europe.

The famous vessel had one more dangerous encounter before meeting its end. During October 1946, near the German coast, she was struck a glancing blow by a floating mine left over from the war. The explosion was amidship, and was strong enough to move the engines from their beds. She was towed to port where repairs were made, and she returned under her own power to Baltimore, Maryland. The ship was laid up there until 1957, when she was finally sold for scrap.

Captain George Anstey, a St. John's Harbour Pilot, has the distinction in Newfoundland history as being the man who brought the *Edmund B. Alexander* into St. John's Harbour on January 29, 1941.

Corbett's Mosquito Fleet

The World War Two Mosquito Fleet of the United States Coast Guard had a close connection with Newfoundland. As matter of fact, nearly that whole fleet was constructed at a one-man shipyard owned and operated by Ed Corbett of Chapel Arm, Newfoundland. The Mosquito Fleet was a fleet of small pleasure boats used to patrol Delaware Bay and the New York and New Jersey coasts. They were sometimes used in battling espionage. The objective of the American Military in developing the fleet was to keep sea lanes open and to strengthen the safety of British and American shipping during war time.

For the production of most of this fleet, the Coast Guard by-passed the largest shipyards in the United States to give contracts to a Newfoundlander's one-man shipyard at Camden, New Jersey. Edward Corbett had by then gained a reputation in several states as an expert builder of small pleasure craft. Corbett had developed his skill while involved in the Newfoundland and Labrador fishery as a young man. He left Newfoundland at an early age and, after working in Montreal and Halifax, moved to Philadelphia in 1922 to work. He found work with the Manshure Silk Mills and quickly worked his way up to Superintendent. This success disappeared when the great depression hit and Corbett found himself out of work.

This plucky Newfoundlander didn't waste time waiting for job opportunities to come to him. He went out and purchased a piece of deserted land on the banks of the Delaware in Camden, New Jersey, opposite the famous Cramp's Shipyard, and began building row-boats. Business was good and he added motorboats to his production. His expert workmanship attracted some of the most prominent residents of Camden and nearby Philadelphia. Newfoundlanders from all over New Jersey, New York and Pennsylvania visited the Corbett one-man shipyard.

Such was Corbett's reputation that when the Coast Guard hit upon the idea of a Mosquito Fleet, they turned to Corbett for most of their needs. Corbett was interviewed by a Camden newspaper in June 1942 and commented, "If I had a gun on my shoulder, I couldn't be doing much more for good old Newfoundland." The article noted that he had developed his skills while living at Chapel Arm and building catamarans and dories. He said, "Right now one of the boats that slid off my ways may be spotting some saboteur climbing aboard a ship anchored with valuable war material for Britain or the United States. Or, who knows, one may be spotting some sub ready to blow allied shipping to kingdom come."

The history of the Mosquito Fleet is revealed in thousands of documents at the Congressional Library in Washington, and very likely this material shows that the Mosquito Fleet did all these things and more.

HMS Calypso/HMS Briton

Sir Roger Keyes, Admiral of Britain's Grand Fleet in World War One, described Newfoundland sailors as "...the finest small ship seamen in the world." The skills and training which these Newfoundlanders displayed so well were acquired through training on what is now a lost piece of Newfoundland heritage, the *Calypso*, which was renamed the *Briton*.

The story of the *Calypso* in Newfoundland is connected with the British tradition of using Newfoundland as a training ground for its Navy, beginning around the time of Sir Humphrey Gilbert's visit to Newfoundland in 1583.

When British troops withdrew from Newfoundland in 1870, there were those in the military who argued that the training of British seamen in Newfoundland should continue. They argued that the program would also provide some military protection for the Colony which had been left defenseless by the withdrawal of the British military.

In 1878, a Captain Sullivan of the HMS *Sirius* put forward a plan for a Royal Navy Reserve Unit and a training ship to be stationed in Newfoundland. The Lord Commissioners of the British Admiralty, who were alarmed at some of the problems experienced by several similar programs in England, refused to approve the proposal. The Lords claimed they had no suitable ships for training boys for the Reserves.

In England at the time was a small fleet of training ships known as Industrial Training Ships, which were privately operated by local groups and financed by public contributions. Several of these vessels were used to rehabilitate and train wayward boys to enable them to follow a seafaring career. These training ships served the Royal Navy well and turned out some of the best sailors in the British Navy.

In 1883, the Royal Navy launched a new warship at the Navy Dockyard at Kent, England which was christened the *Calypso*. The vessel was designed by Sir Nathaniel Barnaby and was the last of the class of ships known as "Steam-Sail Corvettes." It measured 235 feet long, weighed 2770 tons and could travel at a speed of fifteen knots.

The *Calypso* was well armed with four mounted six-inch breech-loaders, two on each side, fore and aft, as well as twelve five-inch breech loaders, six to a side. In addition, there were six Nordenfeldt machine guns on the upper deck and two fourteen inch torpedo tubes on the main deck. Below the main deck was a protective steel deck that could stop all but the heaviest of shells. In 1885 the *Calypso* went into service with the Royal Navy's Training Squadron. By 1898, her career with the Royal Navy had ended and she was destined for the scrap heap.

Newfoundland authorities had not forgotten Sullivan's idea of reviving the colony as a training ground for British seamen. The British finally agreed and responded to efforts to save the *Calypso* by assigning her to the Newfoundland project.

On September 3, 1902, the *Calypso* was re-commissioned as a drill ship. A crew of 167 men was assembled from the HMS *Prince* and the HMS *Vivid* under Commander Frederick Walker to sail her to Newfoundland where the Royal Newfoundland Volunteer Naval Reserve had been organized and were waiting to start training. The RNVNR was created as an Imperial force rather than a Colonial force in recognition of Newfoundland's imperial role in the Commonwealth's defense.

The *Calypso* had a rough trip across the Atlantic and encountered some violent storms. She arrived in St. John's on October 15, 1902. Work began almost immediately to convert the vessel to suit the needs of the trainees. Her fore, main and mizzen masts, and the funnel, were all removed. The flush deck was roofed over with a peaked roof to form a huge floating drill hall. The hull, from which much of her armament had been removed, became the quarters for the Newfoundland Reservists.

When the fishing season ended each year, fishermen from all over Newfoundland went to St. John's to train on the *Calypso*. About 500 Reservists were 'messed' and slept there between 1902 and the outbreak of World War I. When war was declared, the British Admiralty sent out a call for trained seamen, and the Newfoundland reservists were first to respond.

In its 50th anniversary edition 1910B1960, *The Crowsnest*, the magazine of the Royal Canadian Navy, described the Royal Newfoundland Naval Reserves as "...the first really effective naval reserve in what is now Canada." An estimated 2000 Newfoundland reservists served in WWI with about 200 of those lost in action. Another 150 were injured and sent home. Several members were awarded medals and other military honors.

In 1916, the *Calypso* was renamed the HMS *Briton* to release the name for a new fighting ship which was about to be commissioned. The Naval Reserve was abandoned in 1922 and the name 'The Old Briton' survived for decades in Newfoundland.

A. H. Murray Ltd. purchased the *Briton* and used it as a floating salt storage depot. She remained a familiar site in St. John's Harbour for years, frequently surrounded by a flock of small schooners taking on salt cargoes. In time, the salt fishery declined and the *Briton* was moved to Lewisporte and used as a coal hulk. In 1966, in a state of deterioration, the *Briton* was offered for sale.

Author Michael Harrington, a strong advocate for the preservation of Newfoundland's heritage, wrote:

> *But Newfoundlanders were still too new in Confederation to recognize the relevance of the eighty-five year old warship to their now "lost national" heritage. They had already let the last of their "wooden walls," i.e. Scottish-built sealing and whaling steamers of the 19th century, not to mention the "Alphabet" fleet of coastal steamers built for the Reid Newfoundland Company in the late 1898, and the salt fish banking schooners, all slip through their fingers; as well as other craft of varying historic interest.*

Among those who expressed an interest in preserving the *Briton* was Captain Tom Dower of Grand Falls, a sea adventurer who built his own small boats and sailed solo across the Atlantic. Dower purchased the vessel from Murray's with plans of re-rigging her to its original state. When the Government failed to assist the project financially, Dower was forced to drop the project.

The large hulk had become an eyesore at Lewisporte and the people there wanted it removed from their Harbour. In response, Dower sold the vessel to a businessman from Notre Dame Bay who scrapped her and sold the iron and copper fittings, bronze propeller and other parts to scrap dealers.

Dower donated one of her guns and a hand-powered steering wheel to the Royal Canadian Legion at Grand Falls as a tribute to Newfoundlanders who sacrificed their lives at sea in war time. The seafaring tradition carried on by the old *Briton* continues today through the HMCS Cabot Navy Reserves established on September 20, 1949.

War-Hero and Bootlegger

When the captain of the U.S. Coast Guard cutter *Walcott* told the Newfoundland Captain of a rum-running vessel to "Heave to!", he got an unexpected answer.

"See you in hell," said the Newfoundlander who made a valiant attempt to outrun two U.S. Coast Guard Cutters, the *Walcott* and the *Dexter*.[5]

Captain John Thomas Randell was hired by New York mobsters to command their rum-running vessel, the *I'm Alone*. His confrontation with American authorities ended in a six year court battle, during which time, Captain Randell became a famous personality in the U.S. and Newfoundland.

Randell was drawn into the mobster-rum-running operations by a representative of the New York Mob, 'Big Jamie Clarke.' On behalf of his mob-friends, Big Jamie had purchased a schooner called the *I'm Alone* at a Lunenburg, Nova Scotia shipyard. The sole purpose of the vessel was to bring illegal whiskey from St. Pierre, off Newfoundland's coast and Belize, British Honduras to the United States to supply the bootlegging and speak-easy establishments operated by New York mobsters.

Big Jamie paid $18,000 for the *I'm Alone*, which was an impressive looking schooner. It weighed ninety tons, and measured 125 feet long and twenty-seven feet wide. The schooner was equipped with a 100 h.p. diesel engine. To command and take charge of the operation to pick up whiskey and deliver it to the mobsters, Big Jamie sought out an experienced, tough and smart sea captain who was dependable. He found such a guy in Captain John Thomas Randell.

Randell, a seasoned captain and adventurer, served with distinction during World War I in the Royal Navy. He came out of the war a Newfoundland hero. Captain Randell was awarded the Distinguished Service Cross and the Croix de Guerre for his part in a battle with a German U-Boat. He was just the sort of man the New Yorkers wanted in their operation.[6]

After agreeing to take the job, Randell and Big Jamie worked out a plan to minimize the risks in getting the contraband liquor past the Coast Guard. Randell was well aware that the Coast Guard had no jurisdiction in international waters. He agreed to purchase

5. Patton, Janice, *The Sinking of the I'm Alone*, McClelland and Stewart, 1972.
6. The *Evening Telegram*, April 1929.

the liquor cargoes from St. Pierre and Belize and to rendezvous with Big Jamie off the coast of Louisiana. The two men took a bundle of fifteen U.S. bills each, with the middle one torn in half and each one-half-part was placed in the middle of each bundle. The serial number on the half bill became the password to use by each party to identify themselves.

Between his rum-running trips, Randell was often entertained by the mobsters. He was always ready for an invitation to socialize, and always took along an impressive wardrobe. This included a tuxedo, dinner jacket, six dress shirts, twelve dress collars, eighteen pairs of silk socks, several pairs of black leather shoes and a top-hat.

The first encounter between the *I'm Alone* and the U.S. Coast Guard occurred during a delivery of whiskey from St. Pierre to Big Jamie off the Louisiana Coast. The *I'm Alone* arrived at night at the rendezvous point and after the passwords were confirmed, Big Jamie began unloading the whiskey into his motor boat. He was successful in landing one load on shore, and had returned for a second load when, seemingly out of nowhere, the U.S. Coast Guard moved in to make an arrest.

Big Jamie doused his cargo with gasoline, dumped it overboard, and used a flare gun to set it afire. While the Coast Guard was distracted by Big Jamie, Captain Randell made an escape at full speed. He sailed the schooner to Belize, British Honduras, where he continued his illegal operations until March 20, 1929, when the Coast Guard vessel *Walcott* again caught up with him.

Unarmed, the Captain of the *Walcott* went on board the *I'm Alone*, and informed Randell that he was operating illegally, ordering the Newfoundlander to surrender. Randell claimed he was in international waters and the Coast Guard had no jurisdiction to challenge him. The Captain returned to his ship and after a short delay, sent several shots across the bow of the *I'm Alone*. When the Coast Guard gun jammed, Randell used the opportunity to escape. The *Walcott* followed close behind. Gun fire from the Coast Guard during the chase struck Randell in the leg. Serious injury did not result because only rubber bullets were used.

What happened next sparked an international controversy that made newspaper headlines across Canada and the United States. Captain John Thomas Randell was smack in the middle of the dispute which dragged out in U.S. Courts for six years.

The chase continued into the next day. In the Gulf of Mexico, the *Walcott* was joined by a second Coast Guard cutter, the *Dexter*.

Using a megaphone, the captain of the *Dexter* ordered Randell to "Heave to."

Once again, Captain Randell repeated that he was in international water, and beyond the jurisdiction of the Coast Guard. The *Dexter* fired a volley of shots across the bow of the *I'm Alone*, and when it refused to stop, launched an all out attack on the rum-runner. Real bullets ripped apart the sails of the schooner, damaging it to the extent that Captain Randell ordered the crew to the lifeboats. Randell remained on board until the last minute. When the schooner tipped to dive down into the ocean, he jumped into the water, and was rescued by the Americans. One crewman of the schooner drowned during the confrontation.

Once on board the *Dexter*, the survivors were arrested, but treated well. They were given warm clothing, hot coffee and food. Following this, they were taken to New Orleans and placed in jail. When arraigned in court, Randell insisted they were 200 miles outside U.S. territorial limits when arrested by the Coast Guard, and there was no legal right for the authorities to arrest them.

The case dragged on for six years in American courts. It finally ended in favour of the rum-runners. Because the *I'm Alone* was a Canadian-registered vessel, the American Government extended an apology to Canada and paid the Canadian Government $25,000. A total of $25,666.50 in compensation was paid to the crew of the *I'm Alone*. Captain Randell received $7,906, the family of the drowned man got $10,000 and the remaining crew members divided the rest among them.

During the tough economic times of prohibition, some Newfoundlanders turned to the rum-running trade to make a living. Several Newfoundlanders claimed to have worked with the Al Capone organization in Chicago, and were deported from the

Courtesy Kay Coady
Tom Coady of St. John's was employed
on a ship used frequently by Capone. He
is shown here wearing Al Capone's suit.

Al Capone.

United States for their involvement. One Newfoundlander, Tom
Coady of St. John's, had a memorable encounter with Capone on
one of his trips to Halifax.

Coady worked on a Canadian-owned schooner which was
believed to be part of the Capone organization. It was used to ferry
Capone around on some of his visits to the Atlantic area. Coady
was only eighteen years old at the time. He remembered orders
given to him by the schooner's captain regarding expected conduct
while Capone was on the boat.

There was always one or two Capone cronies seated outside
Capone's quarters on the boat. Coady was told to deliver Capone's
meal trays, and then promptly leave. He was only to become
involved in conversation if invited to do so by Capone.
Occasionally, Capone would strike up a conversation. Sometimes,
he and his bodyguards would come up on deck and chat with the
crew.

On one occasion while the schooner was docked at Halifax,
Capone, his bodyguards, and two or three of the crew members,
including Tom Coady, went ashore and ended up at a photo shop.

After Capone sat for a photo, the others followed. That is, all except Coady. When Capone asked him why he wasn't having a photo taken, he replied he didn't have a suit. The gangster was amused by the reply and invited him into the dressing room where he removed his suit and told Coady to put it on and have his picture taken. Coady did. Years later, when one of his children pointed to the picture on display in the Coady family house and asked, "Pop, how come you got a suit on there? You never wear suits."

Coady replied, "You wouldn't believe it if I told you."

The Tsunami at St. Shott's

June 26th, 1864 was a red letter day at least in one part of Newfoundland, for a curious and rather awe inspiring natural phenomenon was apparent at St. Shott's, near Trepassey. It was an unnatural kind of day, threatening some kind of weather most people believed, though what kind they were not prepared to say.

At seven o'clock in the evening, to the surprise and consternation of people at St. Shott's, the sea suddenly began to recede from the shore. It was obviously no mere ebb of the tide for the waterline went out and out and out until it was nearly a thousand feet from the shore. So far did the sea retreat that it exposed to full view the wreck of a British warship, HMS *Comus* hitherto lying submerged in five fathoms of water.

The water went out over 250 yards beyond the wreck of the *Comus* which was seen to good advantage, guns, shot and bolts being plainly visible. Then as suddenly as it retreated the sea returned with great force and speed after about ten minutes and poured in to St. Shott's filling up the Gut with gravel and large stones, overturning several boats and sinking one.

In endeavoring to explain the cause of this phenomenon, the *Morning Chronicle* said:

"No doubt a severe submarine volcanic eruption has taken place somewhere not very remote from the Southern Shore." On the 27th, it was remarked by everyone that the sky had an unusual appearance. It was very sultry, there was a dark, leaden smoke, which seemed to envelope everything and there were loud peals of

thunder and vivid flashes of lightning at the same time. Nothing of
the kind ever happened there before. Masters of ships in port say
that the sky looked like it did in places where they experienced
earthquakes.

Most Unusual Encounters at Sea

Two ships, the *Massasoit* and the *Miranda* sailing in
Newfoundland waters ten years apart, both encountered massive
icebergs which are believed to be the largest ever witnessed by any
ship in Newfoundland waters. One survived the unusual confrontation, the other was destroyed.

Newfoundland history is full of accounts of ships being lost
after going ashore on reefs, running into cliffs and sailing into
rocky coves and bays in fog. The wreck of the American schooner
Massasoit doesn't fit into any of those categories and stands out as
one, if not the only, shipwreck of its kind in this province's history.

The Massasoit

Wrecks involving icebergs usually occur when the ship hits a
submerged spur of ice, or else simply runs head-on into the tower-
ing icy wall. The *Massasoit* was lost after sailing into the big bight
of an iceberg off the Southern Shore in a dense fog during June
1882. This vessel had left Gloucester on June 8 bound for the summer fishery on the Grand Banks of Newfoundland. Her master, a
Captain Bond, had decided to go on to St. John's to pick up provi-
sions. The vessel passed Cape Race on Friday, June 16, and sought
information about ice conditions along the Southern Shore from a
passing Newfoundland skiff. Captain Bond was informed by the
skipper of the skiff that there was no sign of ice. Based on this
information, Captain Bond made no effort to shorten sail and did
not reduce speed.

About twenty or thirty miles southeast of Cape Ballard, the
ship ran into a fairly thick bank of fog, but it was not thick enough
to cut off all visibility. They could still see a short distance in all
directions. The captain maintained speed until after sunset and
took in a little canvas after dark to reduce speed. The vessel con-

tinued at a good speed because of the information received that there was no ice in the area. It was not a very dark night, but the gloomy and grey fog pressed around them.

Neither captain nor crew noticed that the fog was growing lighter and that it was getting whiter than grey on both sides of the ship and ahead. This whiteness was not due to a reduction in the thickness of the fog. It was far more deadly. Unknown to those on the *Massasoit*, they were running into the huge bight or cove of a gigantic iceberg. The brightness on the port and starboard bows and straight ahead was caused by the great iceberg shining through the thinning fog.

Before they realized what was happening, the ship was right up to the head of the bight, and the sides of the bay of ice closed in around them like the cliffs of some rock-bound cove. By this time, the *Massasoit* was moving too fast to be saved. She crashed head-long into the iceberg which was an island of ice more than five miles long. It towered more than six times the height of the schooner's mainmast.

Because the iceberg was so far south, it was starting to break up, and great cakes and blocks of ice, dislodged by the impact of the vessel's collision, came tumbling down into the sea or crashing on the decks. Newspaper reports noted that the southerly wind fortunately was not strong, and it was fairly calm in the bight of the iceberg. Captain Bond and eight of his crew got into one of the dories and rowed away from the stricken *Massasoit*. The newspaper *Newfoundlander* reported:

> *The remaining five men who made up the crew stayed behind to remove some of their belongings. They believed the vessel would not sink immediately. Hardly had the first boat left her than she sunk in a swirl of ice and foam and the five men were never seen again, for the fog closed in and swallowed up everything. Captain Bond and his eight men were rescued and brought to St. John's.*

The Miranda

During April 1892, the *Miranda*, an ore boat, was on a trip from New York to Pilley's Island in Notre Dame Bay to take on a load of copper. By the time the ship arrived at her destination, the captain and crew had an amazing story to tell. They had passed by an iceberg, but not just any iceberg! This iceberg was nine miles long and all in one piece. It reared itself 200 feet above the surface of the water and was 1000 yards wide. The 200-foot height of the iceberg gives an idea of just how big this mountain of ice measured because ice bergs are known to be nine tenths under the water. In this case, the berg would have been 1800 feet, or 300 fathoms below the surface.

The *Miranda* took exactly forty-eight minutes, traveling her normal speed to steam past the island-mountain of ice. According to newspaper reports, the giant berg later drifted south to the Grand Banks where it broke off into a dozen pieces, each of which made very large icebergs.

Bibliography

BOOKS

Angus, W. Mack, Commander, USN, *Rivalry on the Atlantic*, Lee Furman Inc., New York, 1939.

Brown, Alexander Crosby, *Woman and Children Last, The Loss of the Steamship Arctic*, G.P. Putnam and Sons, New York, 1961.

Cardoulis, John N., *A Friendly Invasion, The American Military in Newfoundland 1940-1990*, Breakwater Books, St. John's, Newfoundland and Labrador, 1990.

Dollar, Robert, *One Hundred Thirty Years of Steam Navigation, a history of the merchant ship*, Privately printed for the author by Schwabacher-Frey Company, San Francisco, 1931.

Fitzgerald, Jack, *Beyond Belief, Incredible Stories of Old St. John's*, Creative Publishers, St. John's, Newfoundland, 2001.

Nicholson, W.W.L. *More Fighting Newfoundlanders.* St. John's: Government of Newfoundland and Labrador, 1969.

Mosdell, H.M. , *When Was That.*

MAGAZINES, SCIENTIFIC PAPERS AND NEWSPAPERS

Downhomer, Attack by a sea monster, October 1999, Vol. 12(5), p 85.

Luminus, Search for Nemo's Adversary {re: F. Aldrich's dive in submersible to search for giant squid} Winter 1989, Vol. 15(1), pp. 6-7.

Fortean Times, A birthday gift for Jules Verne (re giant squid at Plum Island, Mass,; mentions 1871-1879 strandings at Labrador and Newfoundland} Coleman, Loren, Winter 1981, (34) pp 37-38.

International Wildlife, Fichter, G.S., Tentacles of Terror {re 1870s giant squid specimens; current research) January-February 1980,   Vol. 10, pp. 12-16.

Atlantic Advocate, Round and About: Monster from the deep (re live giant squid) November 1970, Vol. 61 (3), p. 45.

Newfoundland Quarterly, Giant squid in Newfoundland {covers 700 B.C. - 1967} February 1967, Vol. 65(3), pp. 4-8.

Annual Report of the American Malacological Union, Aldrich, Frederick A. Architeuthis - the giant squid, 1967, pp. 24 - 25.

Financial Post, Morris, Don, Newfie prof probing strange squid (re giant squid), November 6, 1965, Vol. 59, p.25.

Atlantic Advocate, Round and about: giant squid, December 1964, Vol. 55(4), p. 76.

Newfoundland Quarterly, Giant squid story {re. 1877 incident at Portugal Cove}, Winter 1962, Vol. 61(4), p. 15.

Atlantic Guardian, Harrington, Michael F., The sea monsters in Conception Bay (re. Giant squid, 1873, 1877), June 1957, Vol. 14(6), pp. 23-29.

Science Digest, Breland, Osmond P., Devils of the deep {re. 1873 discovery of giant squid}, October 1952, Vol. 32, pp. 31-33.

Youth's Companion, Duncan, Norman, The giant squid of Chain Tickle, September 1, 1904, Vol. 78(35), pp. 404-405.

Atlantic Quarterly

Newfoundland newspapers: *Royal Gazette, Newfoundlander, Public Ledger,* the *Patriot,* the *Herald, Daily News, the Evening Telegram,* the *Courier.*

Toronto Globe and Mail, 1971-1976.

Newfoundland Magazine, St. John's, NL, February 1919, Vol. 2 (5). Title: *Victoria Cross And the White Bay Boy.* Pg 6.

Veteran Magazine, December 1928, Vol. 7 (4) pp. 20-21.

Newfoundland Quarterly, April 1919, Vol. 18 (4), p 26.

Interview with John Ford, St. John's, NL, August 16, 21, 25, 2006.

Interview with Steward Fraser, Conception Bay, April, 2006.

Interview with Kay Coady, St. John's, May, 2006.